"A Day and a Life *describes a ... day at St Alciun's and with it, fifteenth century monastic life... As we observe the monks at their prayers and their work, we glimpse their hearts and their struggles, so similar to our own. Readers of this conclusion to* The Hawk and the Dove *series will enjoy one last visit with their old friends."*

LeAnne Hardy, author of the *Glastonbury Grail* series

"Followers of, and newcomers to, the series are welcomed to St Alcuin's as old friends. Wilcock's prose exquisitely captures those qualities of monastic life which she extols; her narrative is reflective and lyrical, humbly but tenderly evoking the simplicity and faith of a community of devotion. It is a community to which the reader is invited, just as they are, to grapple with what it is to live and love in a fellowship of faith."

Anna Thayer, author of *The Knight of Eldaran* series

Titles in the *Hawk and the Dove* series:

The Hawk and the Dove
The Wounds of God
The Long Fall
The Hardest Thing to Do
The Hour Before Dawn
Remember Me
The Breath of Peace
The Beautiful Thread
A Day and a Life

A Day and a Life

PENELOPE WILCOCK

LION FICTION

Text copyright © 2016 Penelope Wilcock
This edition copyright © 2016 Lion Hudson

The right of Penelope Wilcock to be identified as the author of this work has been asserted by her in accordance with the Copyright, Designs and Patents Act 1988.

All rights reserved. No part of this publication may be reproduced or transmitted in any form or by any means, electronic or mechanical, including photocopy, recording, or any information storage and retrieval system, without permission in writing from the publisher.

All the characters in this book are fictitious and any resemblance to actual persons, living or dead, is purely coincidental.

Published by Lion Fiction
an imprint of
Lion Hudson plc
Wilkinson House, Jordan Hill Road
Oxford OX2 8DR, England
www.lionhudson.com/fiction

ISBN 978 1 78264 200 8
e-ISBN 978 1 78264 201 5

First edition 2016

Acknowledgments
Scripture quotations marked KJV are from The Authorized (King James) Version. Rights in the Authorized Version are vested in the Crown. Reproduced by permission of the Crown's patentee, Cambridge University Press.
Scripture quotations marked NRSVA are from The New Revised Standard Version Bible, Anglicized Edition, copyright © 1989, 1995 by the Division of Christian Education of the National Council of the Churches of Christ in the USA, and are used by permission. All rights reserved.

A catalogue record for this book is available from the British Library

Printed and bound in the UK, May 2016, LH26

*For Deborah Sokell
with my thanks for so much encouragement*

Unless you give up everything you have, you cannot be my disciple.
Paraphrase of words of Jesus, Luke 14:33

He said, "Go out and stand on the mountain before the Lord, for the Lord is about to pass by." Now there was a great wind, so strong that it was splitting mountains and breaking rocks in pieces before the Lord, but the Lord was not in the wind; and after the wind an earthquake, but the Lord was not in the earthquake; and after the earthquake a fire, but the Lord was not in the fire; and after the fire a sound of sheer silence. When Elijah heard it, he wrapped his face in his mantle and went out and stood at the entrance of the cave. Then there came a voice to him that said, "What are you doing here, Elijah?"
1 Kings 19:11-13, NRSVA

Jesus walked, and he stopped. What is the speed of love?
Revd Canon Martin Baddeley, in reference to Jesus and the Canaanite woman, Matthew 15:21-28

In your disabilities and in what you decline to do lies your way home.
Diana Lorence of Innermost House

Gracious and holy Father, please give me intellect to understand you; reason to discern you; diligence to seek you; wisdom to find you; a spirit to know you; a heart to meditate upon you; ears to hear you; eyes to see you; a tongue to proclaim you; a way of life pleasing to you; patience to wait for you; and perseverance to look for you.
St Benedict of Nursia

Also I heard the voice of the Lord, saying, Whom shall I send, and who will go for us? Then said I, Here am I; send me.
Isaiah 6:8, KJV

We're all just walking each other home.
Ram Dass

Contents

The Community of St Alcuin's Abbey	11
Chapter One	13
Chapter Two	20
Chapter Three	27
Chapter Four	34
Chapter Five	41
Chapter Six	49
Chapter Seven	56
Chapter Eight	63
Chapter Nine	69
Chapter Ten	77
Chapter Eleven	85
Chapter Twelve	92
Chapter Thirteen	100
Chapter Fourteen	106

Chapter Fifteen	114
Chapter Sixteen	124
Chapter Seventeen	132
Chapter Eighteen	138
Chapter Nineteen	146
Chapter Twenty	153
Chapter Twenty-One	159
Chapter Twenty-Two	166
Chapter Twenty-Three	172
Chapter Twenty-Four	179
Chapter Twenty-Five	187
Chapter Twenty-Six	194
Chapter Twenty-Seven	205
Chapter Twenty-Eight	212
Glossary of Terms	219
Monastic Day	220
Liturgical Calendar	221

The Community of St Alcuin's Abbey

(Not all members are mentioned in *A Day and a Life*)

Fully professed monks

Abbot John Hazell	*once the abbey's infirmarian*
Father Francis	*prior*
Brother Cormac	*cellarer*
Father Theodore	*novice master*
Father Gilbert	*precentor*
Father Clement	*overseer of the scriptorium*
Father Dominic	*guest master*
Brother Thomas	*abbot's esquire, also involved with the farm and building repairs*
Father Bernard	*sacristan*
Brother Martin	*porter*
Brother Thaddeus	*potter*
Brother Michael	*infirmarian*
Brother Benedict	*main assistant in the infirmary*
Brother Damian	*teaches in the school*
Brother Conradus	*kitchener*
Brother Richard	*fraterer*
Brother Stephen	*oversees the abbey farm*
Brother Peter	*ostler*
Brother Josephus	*teaches in the abbey school*
Father James	*makes and mends robes, occasionally works in the scriptorium*
Brother Germanus	*has worked on the farm, occupied in the wood yard and gardens*
Brother Walafrid	*herbalist, oversees the brew house*
Brother Giles	*assists Brother Walafrid and works in laundry*

Brother Mark	*too old for taxing occupation, but keeps the bees*
Brother Paulinus	*works in the kitchen garden and orchards*
Brother Prudentius	*now old, helps on the farm and in the kitchen garden and orchards*
Brother Fidelis	*now old, oversees the flower gardens*
Brother Basil	*old, assists the sacristan – ringing the bell for the office hours, etc.*

Fully professed monks now confined to the infirmary through frailty of old age

Father Gerald	*once sacristan*
Brother Denis	*once a scribe*
Father Paul	*once precentor*
Brother Edward	*onetime infirmarian, now living in the infirmary but active enough to help there and occasionally attend Chapter and the daytime hours of worship*

Novices

Brother Boniface	*helps in the scriptorium*
Brother Cassian	*works in the school*
Brother Cedd	*helps in the scriptorium and when required in the robing room*
Brother Felix	*helps Father Gilbert*
Brother Placidus	*helps on the farm*
Brother Robert	*assists in the pottery*

Members of the community mentioned in earlier stories and now deceased

Abbot Gregory of the Resurrection
Abbot Columba du Fayel (also known as Father Peregrine)

Father Matthew	*novice master*
Brother Andrew	*kitchener*
Brother Cyprian	*porter*
Father Aelred	*schoolmaster*
Father Lucanus	*novice master before Father Matthew*
Father Anselm	*once robe-maker*

Chapter One

It starts in the deepest darkness of the night. The call of a hunting owl. Across the valley, the loud, melodramatic yapping of a vixen. No other sound. The hens are asleep on their roosts, close together, their heads tucked down. The sheep, packed tight in the byre, breathe air warmed by each other's bodies. The calf sleeps close against the warm belly of her slumbering mother.

The abbey lies under a gibbous moon, rapt in the Grand Silence. Clouds drift. How profound is the night, and sometimes how terrible. Dreams. Death. Darkness. Demons of insecurity, terror, loneliness, regret are let loose. But at this hour, who is stirring?

In the infirmary, small lights burn. The two men who have kept watch over the sick make their second round of the dark hours, quietly and without fuss: turning those who can no longer move, changing wet sheets, checking all is well. Brother Michael holds the lantern up, so he and Brother Benedict can see their way along the passage. The place where they are is eaten by shadows, but the warm, dancing halo of candlelight illumines Michael's face. Even in the crumpled weariness of the depth of night, you can see the kindness. You would trust this man, with your life – and many do. Benedict is new to working through the night. He took his solemn vows – his life vows – in the summer. In his novitiate year, they let him go to bed. But here, someone always has to keep watch. Now Brother Damian has been moved to work in the school, and John is abbot, Michael is grateful to have Benedict with him. And they know each other well. The night strips away defences, and bonds form between man and man, in the care of the sick.

The infirmary is set apart from the main buildings of the abbey: the great church, looming up monolithic, a majestic assurance of faith immoveable under the night wind, the shifting clouds, the waning moon. Beside the church, the cloister garth, and set around its verdant square the west, south, east ranges of the abbey buildings, all folded in stillness.

Father Bernard, the sacristan, is lost in dreams; just the faintest whistling snore. He has no idea what he dreams, because he never remembers them. He is not tortured by the recollection of deadly sweet concupiscence, the sensual ardour of unconscious erotica: not that it doesn't happen – he just forgets. The moon doesn't peep through his window; at this hour she is looking in on someone else.

The sacristan's cell has been built just a little larger, to accommodate an utterly essential device: the clepsydra. This water clock drips time away until the point is reached when the striking mechanism, operated by weights and a rope, turns the axle so that the flail strikes the little bells, and wakes up Father Bernard.

He knows from past experience of embarrassing human frailty what you have to do: get up immediately. The clock will not sound another alarm until he re-sets it for the next night. If he lingers for two more minutes, that can lengthen into three... five... drowsing... back to sleep. And an entire monastic community can fail to make Vigils. This must not happen. So the instant those bells penetrate the sacristan's sleep – and he is listening for them in some buried watchfulness persisting beneath bodily rest – he swings his feet down to the floor, bringing himself to sit upright on the warm hollow of his low wooden bed. And stands up, stiffly, stretching.

Apart from the care of the sick, and the cold nights of early spring when Brother Stephen watches over the lambing, the monastic day begins here, with Father Bernard. He fastens his sandals, his belt. In his cell he has a lantern with a fat candle that burns through the night. Too many abbeys have been rased to the ground as a result of a brother struggling with flint and tinder in the dark. The abbot of this one will not take that risk. So their sacristan sleeps with the light burning, the living flame enclosed securely inside its iron and horn cage. It doesn't stink like the tallow candles of an ordinary home. Monks prize their bees. The beehive is itself a sort of monastery: Our Lady in her chapel surrounded by her industrious virgin community. And the wax burns sweet and clear, freshening the room. If the sacristan breaks wind as he drifts off to sleep, the flame from beeswax restores the air to purity.

Father Bernard takes up the lantern and leaves his cell. Just outside, on a shelf affixed to the wall next to his door, stands the bell, its wooden handle worn smooth and shiny from the hefting of his hand every night of the year.

He starts along the dorter, making the most unholy jangling clamour as he goes by. Unstinting, as he treads slow and reliable along the passage between the closed cells, the faithful hullabaloo rouses the community out of sleep – ker-chang, ker-chang, ker-chang – all the way to the end and back again.

Doors are opening already as he reaches the night stairs. Going carefully, minding his step, one hand holding the lantern, the other clutching the bell, neither free for the handrail, he goes down to the moonlit cloister. He doesn't stop to look through the arches at the beauty of the cloister garth bathed in white moonshine, its shadows and shapes mysterious under the stars; he heads for the abbot's lodge. There he sets down the bell and lifts the latch, picks it up again, and goes through the atelier, stopping outside the inner chamber where the abbot sleeps – ker-chang, ker-chang, ker-chang.

He waits, listens for the sound of the wooden clapper telling him he has succeeded in waking his abbot. Satisfied, he goes out into the cloister, leaving the door open behind him to permit a little more moonlight to shine through, and to save Father John the trouble of groping for the latch of the door in the dark.

By the foot of the night stairs, at the doorway into the south transept of the church, just near the holy water stoup, a stone niche originally intended for a blessed statue makes a convenient place to house the bell while Father Bernard is in chapel. As he places it carefully there, ensuring that the iron tongue so vigorously wagged a few moments before is now hushed, the sacristan is already surrounded by the quietly scuffing feet of the community assembling for prayer. Even given the peaceful monastic tread to which they are schooled in their novitiate years, the brethren descending the night stairs sets up a rumbling like thunder. But here in the stone-flagged cloister, only the ripple and flow of woollen robes and the susurrus of many feet.

Towards the east, in the sanctuary, the perpetual light burns in the ruby glass. High in the rood loft Christ on his cross hangs over this, their world. For a while there is nothing to hear but sandals on stone, robes, the creaking wood of the stalls as men take their places, the discreet muffling of a cough. Then, in the darkness lit only by the sanctuary light, and one lantern, the gathered community comes to absolute silence, ready. The knock of the abbot's ring against the wood of his stall, and you hear them all rise in the darkness.

"*Pater noster, qui es in coelis...*"[1] Abbot John begins the Office. Then the *Ave Maria* and the *Credo*, facing east, turned towards the source of light and hope, Christ the daystar.

"*Deus in adiutorium meum intende.*"[2] The abbot's steady voice speaks into the silence.

1 The Lord's Prayer
2 "O God, come to my assistance."

"*Domine ad adiuvandum me festina*,"[3] comes back the murmur of reply from all around the choir, then the Gloria.

"*Domine mea labia aperies.*"[4] Abbot John again.

"*Et os meum annuntiabit laudem tuam.*"[5]

So the day begins, like a birth, from the dark roots of its depth. So faith walks forward, knowing the prayer by heart, not needing to see. Like an unseen river, the quiet flow of chanted psalms, canticles, and responsories carries the community along its current towards the dawn.

Father Bernard bears the lantern, taking it round, keeping watch. He sees a man drowsing asleep, and gives the lantern into his hand, goes to his own place in his stall. And the sleepy one is glad for the responsibility handed to him, to get up, to take his turn at walking and watching. Sometimes it is the only way to struggle up from drowning in the irresistible waves of sleep.

After Matins, the cardinal[6] Office of Lauds: the *Benedictus* with its antiphon, the prayers and blessings and eventually the *Benedicamus Domino* bringing Nocturns to a close. So they go up again to beds by now well cold, sandals shuffling on the stone, the quiet ripple of robes, the rumble of many men mounting the stairs. Then they give the abbey back to the nightwatch of stars as the moon's remote beauty looks down on them and the great trees ranged about their home sigh in the restless wind.

Back they all come for the Office of Prime in the first uncertain light of dawn. After Prime, the morrow Mass, a pause elapses, spent mainly in the reredorter and taking a quick wash in the lavatorium. Then they break their fast – standing, still wrapped in the Great Silence, just small ale and dry bread now in mid September. Their abbot watches over their wellbeing with

---

3 "O Lord, make haste to help me."
4 "O Lord, open thou my lips."
5 "And my mouth shall speak forth thy praise."
6 "Cardinal" from *cardo*, Latin for "hinge": the day opened with Lauds and closed with Vespers, and thus they are the cardinal Offices.

common sense and compassion; in the winter he sees to it they have gruel seethed through the night over a low fire and doled out into wooden bowls held in hands numb with cold. But yesterday's bread is entirely adequate for this time of year.

Keeping custody of the eyes, eating and drinking tidily and quietly, they stand at the tables. Only the abbot catches the attention of the novice master, signalling a frown of perplexity. Father Theodore responds with the slightest shrug, a barely perceptible shake of the head. He grasps the question his abbot is asking; and he doesn't know either. Yes. Where *is* Brother Cedd?

As the men go from the frater to the chapter house, they leave their ale mugs on the waiting trays at the end of the long tables for the kitchener to collect and wash after Chapter. Theodore steps back from the stream of men passing through, and waits. They are no longer in Silence, and he murmurs quietly to his abbot when John comes to stand at his side: "Shall I go up and take a look in his cell? Now, I mean?"

The abbot nods. "Please," he says.

He marks time in the chapter house as Brother Giles stands ready at the lectern, waiting for the novice master's return. He is looking for the expression on Theo's face as he comes through the door, slips quietly to his place, and takes his seat. Theodore meets his gaze, his face grave – again the slightest shake of the head. Evidently one of their novices has decided to leave them. It happens, and not infrequently like this. A furtive departure without discussion or announcement, as the sun goes down or in the first light of the dawn. His expression sober, Abbot John looks across to the reader, nods his permission to begin.

"... let him not neglect or undervalue the welfare of the souls committed to him, in a greater concern for fleeting, earthly, perishable things; but let him always bear in mind that he has undertaken the government of souls and that he will have to give an account of them," Brother Giles reads out clearly. The "him" in question is the abbot of the community; this one bends his head, looking down at his folded hands. *He will have to give an account*, he thinks, and the burden weighs heavy. It looks like he's lost one.

Chapter Two

"I'm all saddled up and ready to go. Any other messages? Anything else you want me to take?"

The abbot has asked his esquire to go on an errand. Another poor year for harvests, but in the hills where the ground drains well St Alcuin's Abbey has fared better than some. Grain prices are high in the market place, and he wants to send his sister and brother-in-law a sack of oats and a sack of wheat. They have a cow, a goat, chickens, and an orchard. He is entirely sure they will have grown a healthy crop of peas, plenty of onions and greenstuff and garlic, and herbs in abundance. But their land is not extensive enough for grain. He is concerned they may go short, and wants them to have this against the leaner days of the winter. So Brother Thomas is taking the abbot's grey mare. A Percheron, she will carry the extra weight with no trouble at all; and ten miles is not so far.

Abbot John's brother-in-law, William de Bulmer, is capable and shrewd, but his work has been more concerned with management and money than hedging and ditching or mending tumbledown buildings. Brother Thomas has no doubt in his mind that when he reaches Caldbeck there'll be any number of minor repairs that could use the skill of a handy man. There'll be more to this day than dropping off a couple of bags of supplies.

"If you could take just a moment to stop by the almonry and see if Father Gerard has something Madeleine might like – I don't know – a shawl, an apron, anything pretty and useful. And I'll wager both of them would be grateful for a pair of boots."

"In what size?" his esquire wants to know.

"Oh – yes – I have it here – bear with me." From a box on his table, the abbot takes two sets of two woven tapes, pinned together. "The dark one is the length, the lighter one the width. I'm sorry to delay you, Tom; I should have thought of this yesterday."

Aye, you should, thinks his esquire. He is anxious to be on the road, and it irritates him to contemplate how long it might take Father Gerard to sort through their pile of donated boots, to find in the first place one that might fit, and then its mate. But he takes the ribbons John is holding out to him, saying only, "Thank you. I'll be on my way, then. You won't forget to send someone else to help Father Bernard with the laundry?" He heads off towards the door, pauses, turns. "Father John – is all well?" It occurs to him his abbot looks troubled and preoccupied this morning.

"Oh..." The abbot hesitates. He doesn't want to make too much of this. Who knows how it may turn out. "I've lost something," he says. "But no matter. You get on your way."

The almonry opens into the great arch of the abbey entrance, a door matching that of the porter's lodge opposite. From the small room where Father Gerard keeps his records and inventories – what they have received, what they have given – leads a curving stone stairway to the storeroom above. Jesus was right when he observed that the world would never be short of men and women in poverty. As the fourteen hundreds trudge through decades of wet summers, leaving grain beaten down by rain and rotting in the fields, need has never been greater. They do what they can, at St Alcuin's, to lighten the load of the frightened and hungry, the care-worn and cold. Living simply and frugally, no man of them having possessions of his own, working together and pooling skills and knowledge, the community tends to create prosperity.

This is the source of the alms and hospitality they offer all who come to their door, whether beggars or guests. It is the duty of kindness, the practical love that stamps them as belonging to Christ. The woolmark of his sheep that says: "These are mine."

Brother Tom has to smile when he realizes it was William, spending ten days with them back in May, who sorted and organized the almonry store. Father Gerard lives in comfortable disorder, searching vaguely for what he dimly remembers is there. That's not William's style. Muttering, "Set your house in order, man," and a few choice expletives on the side, he tackled the mayhem; categorizing, listing, separating, folding, matching. The late autumn and winter is panic season; just now, at the end of the summer, those who will feel the pinch when the cold comes are not too worried. So everything is much as William left it at the start of the summer. And he has his reward now, because it takes Tom hardly any time at all to find two sturdy pairs of boots, a warm woollen shawl, a fine linen kerchief, and a winter cloak. "Cross them off in your book," he insists – in case William asks if Gerard checked them out properly.

Then, the sun well risen by now, he is on his way. And his spirits lift. It's a fine, warm, mellow day, a splendid day to be ambling along the lanes of England, not footsore but riding in style on this strapping, reliable mountain of a horse. He should make Caldbeck by noon. That will give him a good three hours to turn his hand to helping with any odds and ends that could use his help; and back by sunset, in time for Compline.

He's glad now that he didn't grumble about the extra task of rooting through Father Gerard's stocks in the almonry; it turned out there was nothing to it after all. As he takes in the loveliness of hedgerow and trees in full canopy, in these last few weeks before the frosts come, Tom reflects that it pays not to be too hasty; because you never know. And why make someone feel bad when you don't have to? Why not just be patient, just be kind? If that's the only gift you have to offer, well, it would be a good one. He pats the mare's neck and she signals her friendly appreciation with her ears.

✠   ✠   ✠

In the Chapter meeting, the business for the day is concluded. The novices make their confessions, and leave. The professed brothers make their confessions. Father Francis asks about the arrangements for the tail end of the harvest, which Brother Stephen explains. No other concerns are pressing. The community disperses, about the work of the day.

As the abbot goes to his house, and there sends Brother Tom on his way to Caldbeck, Father Theodore makes his way to the novitiate. Not fast.

Brother Cedd is... where? This – if the absence lengthens into finality – will be the first one Theo has lost. Where is he? The novice master gets up slowly from his place in the circle of seats built into the round walls of the chapter house, slowly he walks across the open space at the centre, the last man to leave, and slowly he walks through the church towards the cloister. He stops by the statue of the Sacred Heart of Jesus. He takes one of the small candles from the pile there. He lights it, using the taper provided, from the lamp Father Bernard set burning before the morrow Mass. Deep in thought, very deliberately, he sets the candle there at the feet of Jesus. He knows it is only a statue, not the Lord himself, just as much as he knows the light he has kindled is only a little candle – it's not his soul, it's not Cedd's soul, it's not anyone's soul, just a candle Brother Mark has made from the abbey's beeswax. But it's all he can think to do, this simple token of his soul reaching out – *where are you, Cedd? My brother, my son. Please,* his heart begs; *please, Lord. At least to know, is he safe? Is it well with his soul? Is he at peace? What has happened?*

Please, Lord. Still he stands there, until from the roots of his love for these young men arises what he really wants to say: *Oh, beloved Lord Jesus; won't you… please bring him home.*

And having admitted this is what he's really asking for, he lets his feet now take him, with their quiet monastic tread, out of the church and into the cloister. Slowly, still.

Theo isn't sure quite how he absorbed the recollection of this way of walking. It's not something his own novice master ever discussed. He doesn't even think about it consciously. But they all walk like this, every man of them. The mindful, deliberate placing of every step, so that their bodies move in a manner conducive to peace, without the bustle of self-importance or the self-advertisement of a confident, open stride. The gait of humility and recollection, the walking of a man gathered quietly into himself; his exterior in the world only so far as it needs to be, his interior an open window. For the rays of Christ's light to shine in. For the Holy Spirit to perch and maybe fly right inside. For the air of heaven to keep fresh the hidden chamber of his soul. Too, there is a stability in this way of walking, as though the monk's feet are touching the sacred earth with tenderness, taking nothing for granted; a man who is properly grounded, to be swayed neither by praise nor by blame. This is the nature of *humilis*, lowliness – the point at which heaven kisses earth. It has to do with feet, and how a man walks through the world.

To this discipline of recollection, add profound reluctance; and you have the measure of Theo's feet walking the length of the cloister from the church, past the abbot's door, along the south range to the day stairs, climbing them to the upper floor, and coming to a standstill outside the door of the novitiate.

His early days in this beloved house, how often he stood like this; one hand on the latch, summoning the courage to open it, always (*Why? How did this happen?*) late. And how has *this* happened, now? Even when he has become the novice master, the man in charge, the one to instruct them, the one whose authority they must obey – still, he stands with his hand on the latch, afraid to go in. Because he knows what they will ask; and when he finally opens the door, treads quietly across to his place in the circle, they *do* ask him. Brother Robert says it (*Aye; you would*): "Father Theodore? Where's Brother Cedd?"

"I don't know," says Theo quietly. And that tells them they must not ask; because if he is gone, then he is dead to them. Sorrow is the native air of death. All loss is grief. So the atmosphere is subdued and their faces solemn as they sit ready for this morning's lesson. Somehow they are not surprised when it turns out the novice master wants them to think about the committed life, about the disciplined outworking of the way they have chosen.

"Because," he says, "the teaching of our Lord in the Gospels is that unless a man gives up everything he has, he cannot be Christ's disciple. Do you see how big that is? Everything. Consider, what might be important to a man?"

They wait respectfully lest this question be rhetorical, but seeing he is actually asking them to come up with something, Brother Cassian suggests: "Wealth – material possessions?"

"The pleasures of human love?" Brother Boniface picks his way delicately to this modest expression of what he means. Then he remembers what the novice master has taught them in the past, about attitudes monks and married people have in common. "Treating someone else as if they were only there to get what you wanted out of them," he therefore adds. "As if they were only tools for your personal satisfaction."

"Power? Like, influence, and having your own way?" Brother Placidus says (he thinks Boniface seems to be going on a bit).

"Status?" Brother Robert knows this is one of the things you might give up to follow Jesus, and at this stage in the journey it isn't yet clear to him whether never having had the remotest chance of any kind of social status in the first place will make the renunciation easier or harder, in the long run.

Seeing most of the things a man might renounce to take the way of Christ have now been spoken for, and he is the only one who has not yet said anything, Brother Felix feels it incumbent upon him to come up with a contribution. So, thinking of his own private struggles, he says tentatively: "Being right?" And that turns out to be a good one; it actually makes the novice master laugh. Everyone breathes easier.

"Yes," says Father Theodore, "all of that. It's about having a quiet eye and a single heart. What the book of Revelation calls our 'first love'. Not that we aren't human; of course we are. But that nothing – absolutely nothing – matters more than this. How I like to think of it is that we are concentrating. You know how Brother Conradus will sometimes boil away water from broth, to get a concentrated stock for a wonderful sauce – one of his masterpieces? That's what this way of life is doing for us, boiling away everything tasteless and unsavoury. We're concentrating. And that means paying attention. Brother Robert, are you all right? Have you got an itch, or are you just bored?"

Chapter
Three

They allocated these two rooms to the novitiate in no random manner. It's upstairs, in the east range, so right at the back of the cloister buildings, tucked away as privately withdrawn from guests as it could possibly be. Since the main work of the day is done before noon, and studying texts forms a central part of work in the novitiate, it is well to have the morning light streaming in through the tall arched windows from the moment the sun climbs above the protective circle of hills behind the abbey. But the seclusion motivated the setting, more than the light.

This is not so of the scriptorium lodged next door. Here, it is critical to see well. Ideally, Father Clement would have liked the true, unambiguous northern light; but since the abbey church constitutes the entire north range, he couldn't have it. At least the eastern light rises earliest. His scribes' desks are set beneath the windows, slanting double lecterns for two men to work opposite each other. Candleholders are affixed to the upper edges of the desks – with lamp-glasses to prevent wax splashing in any sudden draught. The wall furthest from the windows is entirely full of shelves – except for the doorway through to the passage sitting above the corresponding cloister walk below. The shelves contain an abundance of resources both expensive and valuable (not always the same thing). Different sizes of sheets of a variety of thicknesses and quality of vellum. Inks, quills, reed pens, charcoal, chalks, burnishers. A multitude of bottles and stacks of small bowls for mixing gesso and size. Ink horns, knives, pumice stones, rulers, and spikes. Beautiful, almost globular glass bowls to magnify candlelight on a stormy day. Loose pages of books half-finished, or stacked ready for binding. And gold. It is a beautiful, magical place, a treasure trove of curious objects and lovely works of art. The intent, focused quality of its absorbed silence is magnified rather than diminished by the quiet scratchings and scrapings, the sounds of men breathing, shifting, getting up to cross the room, the small sounds of bowls and bottles moved. Nobody who works with feathers and leaf gold, creating wonders, is going to be noisy. Just now and then the silence is marred by someone swearing in frustration; but even that is spoken softly, exasperation in undertone.

Monks are quiet, their voices and movements discreet. Scribes are quiet, their movements careful and precise. Monastic scribes are the quietest of all, disciplined and cautious. There is nothing blatant or rambunctious about these men. Even so, their life does not lack drama. Just now, a tragedy observed but never discussed is playing out its full slow cruelty in their midst; because Father Clement, they know, is gradually going blind.

It has been his desperate hope that the abbot would permit him to train up Father Theodore to step into his place; Theo's illumination is exquisite, and he is the best scribe among them. Father Clement's heart sank when their abbot – not this one, Abbot Columba, his predecessor – announced in Chapter that Father Theodore would replace Father Matthew as novice master. Men in so central an obedience usually either prove disastrous in short order, or stay many years. That day in Chapter Father Clement, with all the composed restraint of a monastic scribe, bowed his head in silent acceptance of his trampled dream.

Not a young man, he was in middle age already when Theo entered the novitiate. He has poured all the ardour of his faith and his passion into creating work of excellence and artistry. He has given his life to this vocation. Knowing this, sometimes in his private prayers and when he makes his confession, he humbly asks for forgiveness that it means so much to him. He understands about the balance to be maintained – the difficult tightrope walk of monastic life – to care enough but not too much. He knows that to receive the gifts of God a man must stretch forth the empty hands of a supplicant; he understands that is what it means to be poor in spirit.

From the outset, from his first days as a postulant, it has been spelled out to him that all he is promised here is Christ and the community. To learn this way of love will ask renunciation of him every single day. He must own nothing, demand nothing, set aside his personal preferences, be content with what he is given. Making peace with disappointment is as familiar to him now as his black wool habit, as his belt supple with use, as his sandals accommodated to the particular shape of Father Clement's feet. Coming here meant giving up any aspirations to making his mark in the world. What mark? When he took his simple vows, he gave up his name. Since then he has been Clement – after that scholar of hungry intellect scented out the trail of learning by here and by there until he finally, under Pantaenus in Alexandria, found rest. And this Clement's abbot in his novitiate days – Father Gregory of the Resurrection – prayed that this talented, eager, passionate young man might also find rest.

Thou hast made us for Thyself, O Lord, and our hearts are restless until they find rest in Thee. So it says on the very first page of St Augustine's *Confessiones*. This, like so many other texts of holy wisdom, has entered deep into Clement's heart and lodged there. He knows the words of the Office by heart – the psalms, the prayers, the responsories. His feet know the paths of the abbey without prompting. His hand finds the rail going down the night stairs for Matins with no fumbling or groping. He is part of everything this life is. He no longer knows the difference between himself and his vocation, so faithfully has he lived it, and for so long.

And even so, the relinquishment of his sight feels unbearable. In the solitude of his cell he goes down on his knees before the crucifix, begging not for special treatment or a miracle but just for a little longer, and for someone to step into his shoes. Until recently there has been nobody. Sometimes the fine lines dance and duplicate on the page; he has to wait and tilt his head, get the angle right. On a good day and in the right light he can manage, but he is no fool. He does not delude himself. It will not be long before he cannot see. But he has this small springtime of hope in his heart that at last there is someone – only a novice still, but showing such promise. Brother Cedd, he thinks, has all the necessary qualities to step into this work. Father Theodore has seen it too, and will advise Abbot John. Clement has never been so presumptuous as to mention this dream he is nurturing; but surely, this time, they will let him have this young man, let him train up this skill. Surely. If he's going to be blind.

✠ ✠ ✠

The abbot's swaybacked grey mare, a draught horse in truth, is bred for strength and steady temperament rather than speed, so Brother Thomas doesn't delude himself he'll be reaching Caldbeck in any tearing hurry, but he's happy with that. It's a beautiful day, the grey is ambling along contentedly, her substantial frame more than capable of carrying a beefy Yorkshireman and a couple of sacks of grain ten miles down the road.

He looks about him cheerfully as they go, enjoying the change of scene. The year is turning. The lady's bedstraw and the hawkweed are finished, and the abundant salad burnet has gone too. But the birdsfoot trefoil, that the lads call eggs-and-bacon for the red and yellow of the flowers, is still colourfully scattering the way, the tiny blue eyebright flowers still peep out from among the grass, the purging flax with its delicate starry blooms, and the witches' thimbles – harebells as they call them, blue as the dress of Our Lady. He keeps his eyes peeled for the brave purple flashes of the autumn gentians – but they don't grow everywhere, though it is their time of year.

He reflects that if he'd had more notice of this visit he might have gone up to see if there were any bilberries left on the moor. He thinks the conditions won't be right for them down in the valley at Caldbeck. He could have picked them some blackberries too – but then they doubtless have their own. Everyone has blackberries. That sets him off thinking about blackberry and apple dumplings with an abundance of cream poured on, and he starts to feel hungry. He wishes he'd brought a hunk of bread and cheese, or even an apple – lovely they are, just now, all juicy and crisp. He's been helping with the harvesting, as he always does, and relishing the liberty to eat as many as he wants – the red-blushed green or yellow; some skins waxy, some rough, the indescribably tart cold sweetness that releases a shock of flavour with the first bite.

He must be half way there. He hopes Madeleine's baked a loaf of bread today. They will have cheese for certain, now they have a cow as well as a goat – and butter. He thinks about snowy goat's butter, such a contrast to the rich yellow of the cow's.

Butter with a sprinkling of salt crystals mixed in, spread thick, melting into torn bread still warm from the oven, with a goodly hunk of that soft cheese Brother Conradus makes – the one wrapped in nettle leaves, and the one rolled in cracked pepper. Or the sharp, tangy hard cheese that takes forever to ripen but is worth the waiting. With plums, maybe. Or what about a cold pigeon leg? Or some stuffed chicken? All washed down with a mug of nice, cold ale.

Maybe Madeleine will have made some pease pottage – it's good at this time of year; it has that delicate flavour while the peas and beans are yet green; before they have been dried for the winter. Now his mouth is watering.

To distract himself from the sense of desolate vacancy developing in his belly, Brother Thomas shunts his thoughts to one remove, reflecting on men he has known who don't seem too fussed about their victuals. Thin, abstemious, fasting men, who skimp on the butter and prefer their porridge with no honey and no cream. Men who shake their head and raise a refusing hand at the offer of a second helping. Men who don't trouble to scrape out the bowl. Such attitudes are, to him, a perpetual source of wonder. But look, now he's back thinking about food again, which he hadn't meant to do.

He's glad that Brother Conradus took over from Brother Cormac in the kitchen. Life improved sharply at St Alcuin's from that moment on. He thinks about the difference it makes who is chosen to fill which obedience. Theodore, for example, leaves Father Matthew standing when it comes to the work of a novice master. He has the knack – or better put, the graces and gifts. And Francis! Tom reflects with interest on the ready smile and irrepressible wit that were forever getting Francis into trouble – too jaunty, too blithe, too chatty, and too charming by half – right up to the point he was made prior. And suddenly, overnight, he began to look like a Godsend – so cheerful, so hospitable, so relaxed in conversation, so likeable. Find the right work for the right man, and suddenly it all makes sense.

This calls to mind a thing Father John said in a recent abbot's Chapter – how vocation is to be worked out in community; "us", not "me". That no man holds all the pieces to the puzzle. That finding and affirming the gifts of each one is what is meant by St Paul's talk of the people of God as living stones, together built into a vital, dynamic, sentient temple of praise. Tom smiles.

"Wick" was the word the abbot used – the old Yorkshire term for something ardently, joyously alive. Like the wick green shoots of the first plants of spring, thrusting through the covering of snow. "Wick". Much as Tom loved Abbot John's predecessor, Father Peregrine, he acknowledges the pleasure and surprise in hearing the simple Yorkshire vernacular in his new abbot's homilies. And he realizes that his instinct to qualify that, with the insistence that nothing could come anywhere near equalling Father Peregrine's teaching or example, is acquiring the slightly faded look of an obstinate response that has had too long a time in the sun.

A curious thing, the loyalties and loves among the brethren, the ties of community. Most essential that they should exercise restraint in this intimate, shoulder-to-shoulder pilgrimage of simplicity. That they lift each other up, bear one another's burdens – to the extent that seems realistically possible – but that each man takes responsibility for a degree of reticence. A living soul has about it a certain solitude. The way of a monk – however vulnerable, however gentle, however loving the man might be – accepts no other conjoining than with the risen Christ. No easy discipline, this. So tempting, at times, to take refuge in something less.

Then he thinks: bearing one another's burdens? Is that even possible? How could you? Give a man a hug when he's feeling wretched, maybe, but bear his burden? What does that mean?

As he rides over the turf cropped short by rabbits and sheep, between these massy outcrops of rocks sprouting thorn trees and little, hard-leaved shrubs, it occurs to Brother Tom that maybe bearing one another's burdens is something to do with being willing to live with the consequences of their ordinary human frailty – the dim-wittedness, the awful table manners, the frightful singing out of tune. And making space for them; overlooking it with kindness. Because everybody needs to be accepted. Even the clumsiest idiot needs to belong.

Chapter Four

The day stairs take you to the angle between the south and west ranges. Along the whole upper floor of the south range stretches the dorter – the community's cells – those of the novices are at this end, in effect next to the day rooms of the novitiate. There's also a door leading to a narrow stone stairway on the outer wall. Convenient to the dorter, it goes down to the reredorter and the lavatorium. Each man has an item of cell furniture for his use in the night, but this easy access to the reredorter is obvious common sense. Beneath the cells in the south range the abbey's store rooms – massive, deep, cavernous – keep their supplies well stocked. Ideally, a food store should be situated at the north end of a house, on the cold side of the building. But here the walls are so thick, the rooms set in so deep, the windows so high in the wall, that everything stays cool enough. The store rooms are situated on the south side to give close access to the river. The cells on the upper floor, each with its tall, narrow window, get the best of the passive solar heat; the men sleep as warm as may be. Not exactly cosy, even so; in the winter some cannot sleep for the shivering cold – "starving", as they say hereabouts, in Yorkshire.

Just now, though, the cells are deserted. In the afternoon, those who need to may take a short rest and many a man will be reading and praying quietly in his cell; but if the afternoon gives opportunity for study and contemplation, the morning is the time to get active things done.

Climbing that stone stairway up from the cloister, instead of turning to the right along the dorter in the south range, Father James, coming straight from Chapter, turns left past the novitiate rooms and the scriptorium to the robing room in the east range.

A massive table fills the centre space. Here he cuts out the black woollen cloth for habits and scapulars and cloaks, and the fine linen for undershirts and drawers.

The abbey walls are of such depth that the windowsills make excellent work surfaces of themselves. Thread, needles, shears, awls, leather, bolts of cloth and everything else he needs, Father James has stacked in orderly manner on the capacious shelves occupying all one wall. A lot of it is black. In another wall is the door through to the scriptorium, where he helps out on days when he has nothing to make or mend here in the robing room. Either side of that door, a run of low cupboards creates a useful countertop. On it, among other odds and ends, is the book where Father James records the measurements for every brother in the community. And in the corner, where the cupboards join the outer wall, stands poised as if she has just landed there an exceptionally beautiful statue of Our Lady Queen of Heaven, masterfully executed, her robes intricately painted in colours rich but soft. She is wearing a most complicated, elegantly contrived golden crown. Her kind eyes, gently glowing complexion, and slightly parted, almost smiling rosy lips grace the daily work of the robing room. She has not always stood here. She was a gift from Lady Agnes d'Ebassier – as was Our Lady of Sorrows down in the chapel. A valuable piece, of considerable artistry, of good size but not immense, the previous abbot's first thought when his benefactress presented her was that if he put that in the church she'd be stolen within the month. Too big for a cell, too pretty for the novitiate, it occurred to him Father James might like her up in the robing room. And he does. Before he came to St Alcuin's, James worked with his father as a silversmith. Almost nothing is too gorgeous for his taste. In this environment of spare simplicity – a place of stone walls, bare wood, humble stools and benches of plain and practical construction, pewter ware and rather basic pottery – Our Lady Queen of Heaven ascended to his work room sweet and enchanting as an exceptionally colourful sunrise. Yes. He loves her. Of course, she has stood there now so long he doesn't always notice her; but still she makes him happy, with her colours, her femininity, and all that glorious gold. And he usually murmurs, "Good morrow, my Lady," as he crosses the room to the window near the corner where she stands, to spread out on the windowsill in the good light his needle-roll or his order list or anything else he needs to examine.

They've had two postulants so far in Abbot John's time, two young men from Escrick, Bernard and Colin. One left after not so very long. What Bernard imagined as a quiet, contemplative, frankly quite easy life, turned out to be tougher than he envisaged. For one thing he was expected to work hard. He was not gently born, but still, scrubbing floors and digging out horse muck had not been on his list of aspirations. And the praying went on so long and happened so often it got beyond boring. Then there were the constant interruptions – doing what he was asked when it was asked of him, without delay, setting any project aside (however interesting, regardless of how crucial a stage he might have reached) when the Office bell began to ring. He hadn't anticipated he'd be required to be that available.

"But... that's what the simplicity of our life is all about," explained the abbot, slightly surprised. "It's not just an end in itself. Living simply, owning nothing – it sets us free. Not to be idle, but to serve, to work, to love. It's the simplicity that gives us to one another. And we give up everything, Brother – everything to which we cling. That's why we move men from one occupation to another. There's a risk of becoming precious and possessive about the work we undertake. The art of freedom and peace is all in the willingness to let go. And that's what makes us available to learn to love – when we no longer have anything to cling to, or defend."

All of which meant precisely nothing to Bernard, and he didn't last long. But Colin stayed. His request to enter as a postulant coincided with a period of some turbulence. Abbot John went through an experience of personal tragedy that knocked him sideways for some while; then the community came to the brink of financial ruin. For men leading disciplined lives of prayer in a quiet place, there seemed to be a lot going on. But eventually the time came that the abbot judged right to accept the two young men from Escrick into their midst. And Bernard left, but now Colin is about to be clothed, and receive his name in religion. He will soon no longer be Colin but Brother Christopher.

"It's a special name," the abbot said to him. "A strong name. You know the story of St Christopher? That the Christ Child asked if he would carry him across the river, and he readily said yes. But he almost didn't make it, because the little lad on his shoulders grew so unexpectedly, unbelievably heavy. It was because – he couldn't see this of course – Christ is carrying the weight of the whole world. He almost dropped him; but he made it through."

And Colin sat in silence, taking this in. After a while, somewhat unnerved, he asked the abbot: "So… why have you chosen that name for me?"

Abbot John laughed. This is something else Colin has noticed – these men have a natural instinct to puncture the bubble of solemnity before it grows too enormous. Just when you are filled with the gravity of the occasion, the importance and consequence of whatever's going down – someone generally cuts it to size by finding it funny. "Don't take yourself so seriously, Colin," the novice master has said to him on a number of occasions: and once (he remembers, now), "Whatever's the matter? By the Mass, you look as though you're carrying the whole world on your shoulders!"

So he hopes – he really hopes – the abbot has not chosen this name for him because he makes too much of an issue out of everything. But that's not the reason.

"What we learn from St Christopher," according to the abbot, "is the necessity to carry no baggage if we want to make it through. He had the bare minimum, the staff in his hand. If we undertake to be Christ-bearers – as Our Lady was, as St Christopher was – we have to really get to grips with understanding that this will cost everything. There is simply no room for extra baggage. There's no room for anything else. That's why we are celibate. That's why we own nothing, why we always look for the humblest and the least. If we try to carry anything else – anything – we won't make it through. And Christopher didn't – take anything extra, I mean; he did make it through. When he stepped out to cross the river, his staff in his hand, wearing only his simple tunic, he took no pack of possessions; he only carried Jesus. And you'll notice, the master asks nothing of the man he's not willing to undertake himself; Jesus wasn't carrying anything either. Well – apart from the whole world.

"Christopher's a good name, Colin; one to think on your whole life long. It's about the connection between freedom, simplicity, and responsibility. It's about knowing what you're getting into, and being willing to keep going. Because there will be moments – trust me – when you can only mutter, 'Hold tight, Jesus! Both hands, for God's sake'; and do your best not to lose your footing. I should think it's a name a man could feel honoured to bear; and it's yours if you want it."

So of course he said yes, though he had to admit it felt daunting.

This morning, when the novice master comes up to join them in the teaching circle at the end of Chapter, Colin catches the sadness and concern in Father Theodore's face before he takes his place among them with his usual smile. This comes as something of a sudden revelation. Until this moment, Colin has always thought of a smile as something that just happens to your face because you feel happy. But it dawns on him today, when the novice master's face a moment before makes it all too clear he is not happy, that a smile – like a friendly word – is a jewel of grace in community. It is the gift of loving kindness, from a man willing to turn away from himself and his own preoccupations, to think about how someone else might be feeling.

It's while Colin is still digesting this insight that Brother Robert pipes up: "Father Theodore? Where's Brother Cedd?"

This has been a matter of discussion among them while they were waiting for their novice master to come up from Chapter. It turns out none of them has seen him this morning. They decide he must be ill, gone to seek out Brother Michael in the infirmary.

When Theo steadily meets Brother Robert's gaze, and says quietly, seriously, "I don't know", they understand. And it sends a shaft of loss right into the heart of them. Brother Cedd. Studious, though not especially scholarly. Humble and gentle. Exceptionally gifted as a scribe. Rarely the centre of any conversation, not the life and soul of the party, the thought of losing him from their company surprises them by the sense of bereavement it brings.

They know they are not supposed to ask questions; this has been explained to them before. Here, they have been told, we cling to nothing. We belong to one another in Christ alone. A man may come and he may go – but all life is a matter of changing and losing. Nothing lasts forever. Let the shock of passing act as a reminder to set your hope upon eternal things. Let it not disturb your peace.

When the novice master turns his gaze upon him, Colin realizes his mouth has dropped open in sheer surprise at the news. He shuts it hurriedly, and again Theodore smiles.

"Colin," he says, "will you go along to the robing room? Father James says he has your robes ready to try."

Colin is not a lad of massive intellect, but even he doesn't fail to notice how the sudden frisson of excitement he feels, sparked off by these words, tosses aside as if it were of no consequence at all his shock and sorrow of the moment before.

He stands up to go. "Yes, Father," he murmurs. As he leaves them to whatever they will be studying this morning, he knows he has caught a glimpse of what Father Theodore is always impressing upon them. They are not to be indifferent, or try to suppress individual temperament – in any case, that would be impossible. Their hearts are flesh and blood, not made of stone. But they must learn to hold steady, passing through the turbulence of life. They must learn not to drop the precious charge of what they have been called to carry, when they must wade through wild waves – whether of accomplishment and success or shame and grief. One minute there will be the cold shock of hearing someone has left them; the next will bring exultant joy for a set of robes. Praise, blame, the regard of others, material prosperity, comfort, health – these can be swept away in a moment; they are ephemera. They must learn to prefer the lasting things, and the things that will make them strong – patience and kindness, faithfulness and humility; the presence of Christ in their midst. They must learn to discern him; sometimes he is there unrecognized, as they will see.

He supposes that this effervescence of excitement, that at last he will be clothed in the habit of the order, cannot be categorized as one of those properties of eternal life he is meant to espouse. Nonetheless, he feels almost giddy with happiness as he knocks on the robing room door. As Father James opens it and invites him in with a welcoming grin, it occurs to Colin to wonder – *Brother Cedd – wherever he is – is he still wearing his Benedictine robes? Or has he ditched them?*

Chapter Five

Colin stands with his arms held out straight from his sides, Father James making sure he's got the sleeve length right, and a comfortable width across the shoulders.

"You can put your arms down now."

He fetches the sturdy belt, and a scrip to hang on it. "Here's your pocket. Keep your handkerchief in it, safe. You'll be having to confess a sin against holy poverty, on your knees in Chapter before the abbot, if you lose that. Here's your rosary. Loop it over – that's right. I haven't got any knives at the moment, but I'm sure Brother Cormac will have some in. I'll make sure we have one for you in time for your ceremony."

He brings the scapular from the table, and lifts it over the young man's head. The sides are tabbed together, but loosely, so Colin will be able to get his hands in and out, reach his hanky, his rosary, his knife. Father James steps back and inspects him critically, nods in satisfaction. "Good. Perfect length."

The cowl likewise sits on him well. Father James knows he mustn't show off about his craftsmanship, and the young men he kits out in their robes rarely comment. They usually stand (like this one) almost overwhelmed by the privilege and wonder of reception into the monastic order; thinking about their vocation, not about his stitching. In fact, Father James can't think of one single postulant whose first thought has been, "My word, Father

James! Black linen thread on black wool, in all these short days and lowering weather, and you managed these wondrously straight lines of such amazingly tiny stitches? Man, you're an artist of the first water!" Or his second thought, for that matter. But never mind. Our Lady Queen of Heaven is watching: offer it up, and what more can you ask?

Father James ascertains that Colin knows what will be happening.

"Father will receive you in Chapter – you'll be tonsured first. Father John used to be our infirmarian, so he's nifty with a razor, you'll be fine. You'll be wearing your regular tunic, but the chemise I've made you underneath that. No need to be as all-for-God as Francis of Assisi and strip to the buff. So then you lay aside your tunic and kneel before the abbot, and he dresses you in this lot that I've made. In silence. After that he gives you your new name. Has he said what that's to be?"

"Christopher."

Father James pulls an admiring face. "That's nice. Swimmer?"

He gestures towards the table, where a nondescript stack of black wool lies neatly folded. "That's your other set. You'll have two of everything. We do give you boots, but unless the ones you have are outlandish in some way – which I see they're not – you can keep those that you've got now until you need new. Saves on cost.

"Good. Right, then. Let's have those things off you, and I'll put them by ready. You know all the other bits that happen? You have to promise you aren't married and you haven't got any incurable disease – and there's the blessing and censing of your robes, the presentation of the Rule and your promises and everything. Father Theodore been through it all with you? Not yet? Well, he will. It's any day now, isn't it? Thanks – don't worry, I can fold it for you. Brother Christopher, eh? Good. That'll sit well on you."

Colin feels vaguely out of his body as he drifts to the door, his mind expanded into the magnitude of what he is about to undertake. A lifetime of celibacy. What? Nothing to call his own, ever again. Swearing absolute fealty to the abbot – and Father John occasionally looks more than grim. But this... he doesn't understand why something deeper than his viscera reaches out for it so ravenously. This – he has glimpsed it in the brethren – this way of faithfulness and self-control is like a mountain spring. Like sweet water bubbling up from mud and rocks, so peace and joy emerge from it. He – everything in him – wants this.

With his hand on the latch, suddenly he remembers his manners and turns, blushing. "I'm so sorry," he says humbly: "I forgot to say thank you. Not – I hope you know – not because I'm ungrateful. It's overwhelming. Thank you, Father James – thank you so much."

And James is laughing at him, amused at the excitement and exaltation. "God bless you," he says. "Welcome to the family. Ooh – could you drop this in to Father Theodore for me? Father Gilbert asked me would I bring it up to him after chapel this morning, but I forgot. And he asked, could you and Brother Cassian and Brother Boniface stay in choir after None, to go through some of the music for next week? He said he looked for Theo – er, Father Theodore – after Chapter to ask him, but he couldn't see him."

Colin looks at him, and Father James says, "Is that all right?"

"Oh, aye, indeed. Me and Brother Cassian and Brother Boniface. I'll ask permission." He thinks it better to keep to himself the thoughts passing through his head, trying to imagine being on such familiar terms with his quiet, serious novice master. *Theo*. It gives him a glimpse into a whole different web of relationships.

Colin takes the Mass setting held out to him, and Father James, with a friendly grin, waves him goodbye.

The robing room is only two doors along from the novitiate, but these work rooms are large – it's quite a length of corridor. As he walks along clutching the book to his chest, Colin practises walking how Father Theodore showed him.

"The trick of it is" – this is how the novice master put it – "to pick your feet up rather than put them down, if you see what I mean. Not splat-splat-splat like a flat-footed overweight alewife, and not striding along like a knight of the realm with your heels striking sparks from the flagstones. This is God's earth and you're walking softly on it. Your tread must become a humble touch; gentle. No swagger, no braggadocio. There should be a concentration of quietness and humility emanating from your presence like smoke from incense – and it shouldn't be billowing out so intensely silent and self-mortifying that the fragrant clouds of it choke everyone to death, either. Just gentle. Just calm. Just at peace."

It sounds lovely. He tries this walk, and feels a bit self-conscious. He thinks he probably looks more like his feet have blisters. Father Theodore didn't mean hobbling. Looking round to make sure no one is watching, he nips back to the robing room door and tries again. There is a plantedness, a sort of supple heaviness in the way the solemns[7] walk. He strives to capture it, can't, wonders if he ever will. Maybe you need to actually feel peaceful to achieve it. Or maybe achieving it is a way of walking towards the peace. He doesn't know; but reaching the novitiate door for the second time, he thinks he'd better go in.

He has been somewhat in awe of the novice master, but... *Theo*. Perhaps that day will come to him too. Somewhere far into the future, perhaps that's what he will say. And what will they call him? Chris?

✠ ✠ ✠

---

[7] Solemns – professed brethren – monks who have taken their solemn (life) vows.

Frumenty. Served by his mother's hands, with roast pheasant and onions, plenty of herbs, it was pleasant enough. It made a change from bread and filled up a lad's belly – very welcome.

Then he had entered monastic life when Brother Andrew held the obedience of cook, and he made frumenty too. But he had different ideas about it. Onions, yes. Boiled. Herbs, to a certain extent. No salt, because it was expensive. Sometimes a bit runny, like porridge, sometimes a dollop that needed a whack from the server to shift it off the spoon into a man's bowl.

And then, Lord have mercy and deliver us, sixteen years with Brother Cormac's cooking. Now, his rendition of frumenty was something else altogether. How does he do it, Brother Tom used sometimes to wonder; how does he contrive to make cracked wheat lumpy? The man has a sort of genius, headed in all the wrong directions. And herbs? Nothing out of a recipe, mind – *any* herbs. Anything fresh, anything dried, whatever he had in store. Dill and mint and a few cloves chucked in because the pepper had run out? Fennel seed and cumin seed and a good old branch of rosemary (because it grew aplenty) to ramp up the flavour? Salt? Maybe. Sometimes he cooked it in wine, sometimes in some broth he had left over. He'd even bung in a handful of fungi from the woods if the mood took him. No one but Cormac thought eating mushrooms could be any kind of a good idea; heaven knows, men have died from eating mushrooms. Besides which, if you don't get them fresh they can be crawling with maggots.

Father Peregrine was an inspired man for simplicity and following in the way of Jesus; and in no respect did he carry out his vision more radically and powerfully than appointing Brother Cormac as St Alcuin's cook. Sixteen years. Glory be to God, that must have made us holy. If that hasn't knocked every brother a decade off Purgatory, there can't be anything would.

But then… oh manna – a salvation of sorts; along came Brother Conradus. And when he makes frumenty, it's a different story. Oh, sweet mother of God, Brother Conradus's frumenty! It has honey, it has cinnamon, it has almonds, it has milk, it has cream – aye, and butter. It has nutmeg grated on it. It's not slack and runny and bitty, it's not solid and stodgy – it's cooked to perfection... what's that Latin word? *Dolce*. Describes Brother Conradus's frumenty to a T.

Every brother of the house has had need to let his belt out a notch or two since Abbot John let Brother Conradus loose in the abbey kitchen. And life is pleasanter, and the men are more cheerful. It's nice having a supper you can look forward to, on a cold, wet day. It makes life better to know the butter won't be rancid, and you won't be having to ignore bits of blue mould on the bread.

The only thing about it is possibly meal times can loom larger than they should. There are times, now, when the north-easter blows frigid off the moor, the days are dark and the nights bitter, when supper is actually the highlight of the day. Who could make a case for that being admirable religion? But what I wouldn't give for a nice big dish of Brother Conradus's frumenty in front of me now. I wonder if this mare is hungry? I wonder if there's a difference from hay to hay? If some of it's more like Brother Andrew's suppers, and some of it (God save us) resembles Cormac's? And if there's some kinds of hay, all green and fragrant with herbs, a distillation of summer, that correspond to the wonders Conradus dishes up? Horses like grain. I wonder – suppose they were hungry – if they'd eat frumenty? At least just give it a try?

All the while these ramblings drift and swirl through Brother Thomas's mind, the sturdy grey keeps her leisurely pace, carrying him through the beautiful hills and dales of North Yorkshire, through the mellow, golden warmth of this September day.

And at last – a bit saddle-stiff; he doesn't have any call to ride out this far so often these days – Tom recognizes the long, narrow lane that runs like a riverbed between tall, graceful, over-arching trees, and describes a curve to the right; then there's the silvered oak gate of Caldbeck Cottage. Right welcome sight, and none too soon. He can't actually swing his leg back to dismount from this horse with two sacks of grain up behind him. He urges her close to the gate, and reaches down to flip over the heavy iron latch; then it pushes open easily.

Within the barest minute, the cottage door opens and out comes the abbot's brother-in-law, William de Bulmer; thirty years a monk, now a householder.

"Well met!" he calls out in surprise. "I wasn't expecting you! What's brought you here? No trouble, I hope?" He laughs. "Oh, I see – you can't get down; let me heft these off for you. Whoa! Steady, girl!"

Brother Tom explains that for once no searing tragedy has befallen them – John simply wanted to be sure they had some grain in store and wouldn't be worried about facing lean days in the winter.

"Not that he doesn't think you provident – don't take me wrong. He thought you'd be well off for peas and eggs and cheese; just maybe having to pay these high prices to get grain from the market."

"That's thoughtful," says William. "That's kind. God reward you. Will you come round with me to the stable? If I give this lass a rub down, would you fetch her a pail of water from the well, yonder?"

So they settle the mare comfortably with a drink and a net of hay, then stroll back to the house.

"We…" William hesitates. "I expect I'd better tell you before we go in. We have something of yours."

Brother Tom looks baffled. "Something of mine? That's clever work, seeing I don't even have anything to call my own."

"Aye, well, I think you'll call this your own."

Further puzzled by this cryptic reply, Brother Thomas follows

William through the house door which opens directly into the big room where they eat and cook and work and read and relax. The room with the huge fireplace with its iron pot slung on chains over smouldering embers. With the comfortable, scrubbed oak table on which bread and cheese and ale and fruit (welcome sight) have been set out.

And there, at the table, half-rising from his stool in dismay, aghast to be greeted with the unexpected sight of the abbot's big, burly esquire, the tense form and blanching face of Brother Cedd.

Chapter Six

When Colin comes back from the robing room, he feels conspicuous in his layman's garb; not so different, after all, from the tunics the novices are wearing – but the tonsures, the scapulars, the rosaries, the uniform black, all set them apart. He longs to be admitted to this exclusive communion, with its aura of dedication and holiness. It's strange and lonely, the place of a postulant. He has expressed his desire to leave the world of ordinary folk going about their normal occupations to be part of this, so that severance has occurred in his will, in his expressed intent; but he is not yet one of them. And all the others are careful to call each other Brother Cassian, Brother Boniface, Brother Placidus, Brother Felix, Brother Robert – where he has to be just Colin. The day of his clothing can't come soon enough.

He gathers from the conversation, as he enters the teaching circle and takes his place, that Father Theodore has been allocating duties for the week ahead. Colin indicates the score that he replaced on the shelf as he came in, and relays the message from Father James about singing with Father Gilbert in the afternoon; and Father Theodore nods and gives his permission.

"Now you're back, then, Colin, let's begin our lesson. I wonder can anyone tell me, literally I mean, what is monasticism? Where does the word come from? What is its origin? What language?"

Uncertain silence greets these questions; but they all know

they can rely on Brother Felix. "It's Greek, isn't it, Father? I'm thinking of Aristophanes' play, *The Birds*. It has monopods in it – people who have only one foot. And monotonous – when someone has no variety in their voice but speaks all on one note. So, something to do with the practice of... well, being one, I suppose."

Colin looks at him in astonishment. How does he know all this stuff? He looks at the novice master and sees the lively interest in his eyes, the response to something intelligent being said for once. Colin seriously doubts that anything he could possibly say would spark that same glow of interest. Now he thinks about it, he remembers Brother Cedd saying something similar only a few days ago – that even if he scraped the bottom of his mind so thoroughly he began to chisel into the actual wood, he'd never dredge up any observation as intelligent as the things Brother Felix comes up with.

"That's entirely correct," says the novice master. "Monasticism began in the desert, and the word expresses something of that – the practice of being alone; solitary, set apart. The Greek is μ☐☐☐☐ – *monas* – as I'm sure you all know. It means 'unit', and is in turn derived from μ☐☐☐☐ – *monos* – meaning 'alone'. If you put those together and think about it, you could argue that it's also about the practice of becoming one; of drawing apart to create new unity. Community, in fact – being one with each other.

"Now, from the same root grows the word *monad* – also Greek. It came from Pythagorean thinking, and it was a term for the first being, the source for all beings, the origin of all being. The monad is divine. Before the monad there was nothing, and if we trace back through the whole tree of life to the primal root, the original being, that's the monad. In our vocabulary, what would that be?"

"God," says Brother Robert, but thinks he's probably wrong when Brother Felix says, "Christ."

"Say more, Brother Felix."

"I'm thinking about the Gospel of John, how in the beginning was the Word and the Word was with God, and the Word was God; and without him was not anything made that was made. And that is Christ, in his cosmic perspective."

"Thank you," says the novice master. "Yes. Can you – all of you – see, then, that the word 'monasticism' has a whole lot more inside it than simply meaning 'alone'? It may have meant that, to express the drawing apart into solitude of the desert fathers, who all lived as hermits in caves, but it also bears inside it an association with the divine, with the Logos, the origin of all life – and with being one. Who remembers where Christ prays that we may be as one – completely one, as he and the Father are one?"

This time Brother Cassian is hell-bent on preventing Felix from having all the glory. "John 17," he says quickly. "The big long prayer on the night before his death, after the Last Supper."

"Yes," says Father Theodore: "and what does Christ say and do at the Last Supper? Colin? Do you know?" He speaks gently, and his eyes are kind; from this Colin discerns the answer must be something easy, but he's so nervous about being asked anything that for a moment he can't think at all. He tries to shut out the look of faint incredulity on Brother Felix's face. "It's how Brother Cedd put it last week," he says at last: "I think I must be just such an idiot."

Father Theodore frowns. "He said you were an idiot?"

"No. He said he was."

The novice master looks at him thoughtfully. "Well, you aren't and nor is he. If I remind you that the Last Supper was the occasion of the institution of the Eucharist – does that jog your memory?"

"Oh!" says Colin. "Right! He broke the bread and poured out the wine, and he said, 'Do this to remember me.'"

"Exactly so. Let me try and put these things together for you.

We have the monad, the divine original being from whom all creation proceeds. In the Gospel of John, we have Christ the Logos, the living Word proceeding from God, and without him was nothing made that is made – all things came into being through him. So John is identifying Christ as the monad; Greek thought systems at work. It's why we call him the 'only Son' of God. If we look at the French, that helps us – *fils unique* – the only son. Do you see? This idea of singleness, of the *only being* quite like this, associated with Christ? Then, still in John's Gospel – and that's important – we have Christ's prayer that we may all be one *as Christ and the Father are one*. Why it's important that this is in John's Gospel is because of the prologue identifying Christ with the monad. This is a huge idea John is importing: the implication is that by our love – our *agape* love for one another in community – we will be taken up into participation of the divine.

"So then, look at Christ's words at the institution of the Eucharist – which we also call 'communion', being made one. He breaks the bread, he pours out the wine – 'This is my body,' he says, 'this is my blood.' So now we have an image of something scattered and torn, fragmented, spilt, dismembered. Remember what I taught you about the Didache – the earliest catechism? How it says concerning the broken bread, 'As this broken bread was scattered over the hills, and then, when gathered, became one mass, so may Thy Church be gathered from the ends of the earth into Thy Kingdom'? Look at it, brothers, think about it, see what's going on. Christ says, 'Do this *to remember me*', to make me one again.

"It's about unity and brokenness, about the origins of life held together in unity, then the scattering and fragmentation caused by violence and sin, then the healing – the shalom – of unity rediscovered in love, in our life together, in the monastic way."

"'God was in Christ,'" quotes Felix in soft and reverent tones, "'reconciling all things to himself.' That's… I can't remember if that's in Corinthians or Colossians, Father."

Thank God there's something he can't remember, thinks Colin.

"Because it's both," says the novice master. "The fifth chapter of second Corinthians and the beginning of Colossians.[8] And yes, that's the point. The whole purpose of the monastic life is to express the divine principle at the heart of creation: unity with one another and with God, reconciliation, single-heartedness, undivided by particular friendships or carnal loves. Is that… am I… do you understand?"

There is a sudden plea in his eyes. These things that set his soul on fire, he so wants to communicate them. The circle of young men look back at him and, even though it is small, it includes those who understand him perfectly and love the theological and philosophical integrity of it, those who glimpse and then lose sight of what he's teaching them, and those who haven't a clue what he means but would never dream of saying so because they love him and he'd be so disappointed.

"Augustine," says Brother Felix: "'the Body of Christ – I Am'."

"Exactly!" Father Theodore always speaks quietly, but Colin notices he can pack some passion into what he says sometimes, even so. "Yes, *exactly*."

In the impressed silence, Brother Cassian clears his throat. "So – Father – is there something we have to do about all this? I mean, does it have a practical application? Or is it just part of the workings of faith and divine mystery?"

"Oh, it's practical." The novice master nods enthusiastically. "It's not meant to be all above our heads, just a scholarly exercise. Nor is it all about being clever and being right. That's not what Jesus was interested in. It's for the healing of our souls and the creation of joy, of peace. To become one requires a lifetime's

---

8   2 Corinthians 5:19 and Colossians 1:20

practice and effort. We try, we stumble, we fail, we get it wrong, we come back and try again, we understand, we forgive, we help each other up. It requires of us the exercise of patience and kindness, of self-control and humility – gentleness. And it asks faithfulness of us. We won't get there unless we are faithful, simply because Rome wasn't built in a day and neither is the kingdom of Christ.

"Though I've heard Abbot John say in a homily – it was a new thought to me, and I think he's quite right – that we just have to turn the key, open the door. He connected up the words of Christ from the book of Revelation, 'Behold, I stand at the door and knock',[9] with the words of the thief on the cross, 'Jesus, remember me when you come into your kingdom'.[10] He said that in the same way as we re-member Christ in our communion, so Christ re-members us in the coming of his kingdom. We are healed, we are made one with each other, we regain our integrity as his kingdom comes on earth. But Father John said that when he asked himself, where *does* Christ come into his kingdom, he realized that it happens wherever and whenever we say he can. He stands at the door and knocks. We just have to open it. So it's true both that this process takes a lifetime, and that it's the gift of a moment. And maybe, after all, a lifetime is made up of a sequence of moments giving us the chance to say 'Yes: come on in'."

And then the thing that every time reminds Colin why he loves Father Theodore. Suddenly uncertainty comes into the novice master's face. He falters. He looks anxiously round the group. He says, humbly, "I'm sorry. I think I've gone off on a pet hobby-horse of my own. I've been talking too much, haven't I? I expect you have much better ideas than mine. And now it's time we were packing away ready for the Office. Remember – Brother Cassian, Brother Boniface, Colin – Father Gilbert wants to see

---

[9] Revelation 3:20
[10] Luke 23:42

you in the choir after you've eaten. But Colin, I need you to come up and see me first – just for our routine conversation. Thank you, brothers. I'm so sorry I went on so long."

Colin, reflecting on this as the novices go along the upper corridor and down the day stairs to the cloister together, thinks how curious it is that while he feels so much in awe of his novice master, there's something about the man that makes him want to give him a hug sometimes, just to reassure him.

Chapter Seven

Father Bernard has felt unhappy about this since he first had to do it. Years have gone by, nothing has improved. The problem has even been compounded by passing time, because if you do anything long enough it becomes tradition, it acquires a strength of its own. You tie a man with one linen strand and he can snap his bonds without the slightest effort. You wind the same strand round him a hundred times and you have a prisoner. There's strength in habit. What you do every day becomes who you are. And that's the whole problem.

It all started back in Abbot Columba's time – whom they called Father Peregrine. To be fair, Bernard wasn't sacristan then; that only started when Father Chad held the reins between abbots. Back in Father Peregrine's time, he'd been sent as a novice to help out Brother Paulinus – and somehow got stuck with it, even after he'd been ordained and Father Chad made him sacristan. Bernard hoped he'd only have to do both jobs for a while, until they got a new superior in post.

And now there's Abbot John, who apparently hasn't noticed how extremely unreasonable and unfair this is; at any rate he shows no signs of doing anything about it. Father Bernard wonders if he can raise the matter. Not really, he thinks, seeing his only objections are that he's sick of it, has enough to do already, and doesn't see why someone else shouldn't take on the job for a wonder. He suspects that on those criteria he could be the first in a very long queue asking for a change. The abbot himself doesn't always look entirely overjoyed with the obligations his role places upon him.

There is something else, though, and if he's honest (which just now he's trying to dodge) Father Bernard knows this is not altogether admirable: it's that he thinks, as an ordained man and the sacristan at St Alcuin's, being expected to do the laundry is, frankly, beneath him.

It's not that he has no help. Someone usually spares one or two of the novices from their regular occupations. Brother Cassian occasionally helps if the children aren't in school – when they're out picking the plums or the cherries. Brother Robert often comes over; there are natural spaces between jobs in the pottery. Brother Cedd hardly ever shows his face when there's washing to be done; though, thinking about it, poor Father Clement is squinting badly these days. He's relying on that lad, training him up in the fastest possible time. You can't blame him wanting to make the most of what eyesight he still has. Now, Brother Boniface is a frequent assistant – because candidly he's of little use in the scriptorium, but he delivers a mighty beating to a linen sheet with a paddle. Good thing he's not left overseeing the schoolboys. And Colin, the new lad – ah, good value there! A hard grafter, no airs and graces; not like that Brother Felix.

Father Bernard, if he had to suggest someone else to take on responsibility for the laundry, would put forward Brother Richard. The fraterer's work can't possibly be as onerous as a sacristan's duties; he doesn't have to be up first in the middle of the night and again at dawn, for one thing. And a fraterer's work isn't so lofty. There's not such a jarring contrast. What does the fraterer have to do, after all? Keep the whetstone and sand in good order, all tidy and ready in the lavatorium for the brothers to sharpen their knives. Set the table and clear everything away after meals. Make sure there are water jugs supplied and filled at mealtime – and ale. Work with the kitcheners to get the bread to the table, and the bowls of condiments – which have proliferated since Brother Conradus took charge in the kitchen with his conserves and pickles, his chutneys and mustards, and the good Lord knows what else. He has to change the towels but that's only once a fortnight, and the last abbot put a stop to tablecloths – said they went beyond the boundaries of holy poverty – so he hasn't got to bother with those. It's the fraterer's obedience to see the towels washed and repaired, but at the moment Brother Richard tosses them in with the rest of the things – as Father Bernard sees he has done today. He has to sweep the frater, of course, and the adjacent paths and cloister passage, and strew the floors with fresh herbs. He has to keep the lavatorium clean – so laundry should come naturally to him. But how long can those chores take a diligent man?

It hardly compares with his own responsibilities as sacristan. He's the timekeeper for the whole community for one thing. The sacristan's is a high-ranking office; he has to be a priest. He has to care for the candles and light them, scour the sacred vessels every week, bake the hosts, launder and iron and fold the corporals – which shouldn't cause *any* man to say, "Oh well, if he's doing that he might as well take on the rest of the laundry while he's at it."

So now, because it's Tuesday, he has to take the barrow and collect all the dirty linen from the big chest by the bottom of the night stairs, and cart it along to the laundry room to be scrubbed. Thank God they at least wash their own braies. Half the men put out their sheets this week, the other half the following week. It's a big load.

The water running into the laundry troughs is clean and pure. It comes from two springs high up in the hills, piped along lead-lined masonry conduits and passing through cisterns allowing sediment to settle and pressure to build. The laundry is warm (if oppressively steamy) from the fires under the big brass water pots. Father Bernard grudgingly concedes he should be grateful; at St Alcuin's he doesn't have to kneel at the water's edge and scrub the sheets in the river shallows – at least their system is properly organized. And Father John lets them have the good olive oil soap all the way from Italy. Bernard still remembers the stink of the soap his mother made from lard when he was a lad. This is much nicer, and scented with Brother Walafrid's herbal oils furthermore – lavender and rose, rosemary and lemon balm. Right round the edges of the drying green behind the laundry room, where Father Bernard spreads the sheets to dry in the sunshine, latherwort is growing in abundance. Well organized, true, and well provided for – but there's no getting away from it, this is back-breaking work. Especially because Father Bernard is tall. The stone troughs and their slanting stone scrubbing slabs are that bit too low. By the end of the morning he will barely be able to straighten up. He knows that already. Tuesday is not his favourite day.

When he gets to the laundry with his mountain of linen, he can hardly believe his eyes. No one has come to help him. The water is heating – Brother Richard lights the fires early on while Bernard is still busy in the vestry – but now he's gone, and there's nobody around. It is physically possible to tip the water from the cauldron into the trough without help – whoever built the place thought of that when they sited the firepits and the washing troughs – but it certainly isn't easy, and Father Bernard has scalded himself on that manoeuvre more than once. He could also do with some help to haul the wet things that have been soaking in lye to be rinsed off and washed through. They get so heavy.

He stands in the middle of the laundry room feeling immensely sorry for himself for some little while. It looks as though there really is no one coming to help him. He thinks of going to look for Brother Richard, but if he's honest (and he's still dodging that) the sense of absolute martyrdom has a sort of horrible addictive sweetness he's half enjoying. He thinks he'll struggle on alone. This is his cross to bear. This is what people are like. Where is help when you need it? What's the point of all the fine talk about faith and dedication if you can't even see to it there's someone on hand to help with the washing? Call this a community? Huh. Moodily, he shoves the plug into the drain, and lets the water begin to accumulate in the big stone trough.

He fetches the bats and the soap, rolls up his sleeves and fastens them back, tucks the hem of his tunic up out of the way into his belt, ties on a big linen apron, soft with wear and many times patched, and starts to pile half the linens he's brought along into the trough.

Struggling and sweating, his hands double-wrapped in rags against the heat of the metal, he tips the hot water into the trough. He bungs the hole where cold water flows in. It doesn't back up and flood – that's the point of the cisterns; their capacity is enough to regulate the system.

So he begins, his red, wet hands scrubbing and slapping the linens viciously on the grooved stone slabs. He repents of that fairly quickly; he knows perfectly well the way he's going at it could rub the sheets into holes there and then, and linen is expensive. He pauses, stands quite still, discreetly smites his breast with his soapy fist, muttering "*Mea culpa.*" He comes back to the scrubbing more gently; but there's nothing to stop him smacking the hell out of the wet linen with the bats.

In a weary pause, as he stretches his aching back and wipes the sweat off his brow with the corner of his apron, he hears footsteps approaching. Oh! *Now* they turn to, when the job's half done!

He bends to the trough again so that they'll find him hard at work and all alone when they come through the door. And then it's his abbot's voice saying, so humbly and full of concern: "I'm so sorry, Father Bernard, please forgive me. I didn't remember until just now that Brother Thomas was meant to be helping you with this today. I sent him out on an errand first thing, and promised to look out somebody else to help you, and I completely forgot. I am so sorry. Here – let me help. What shall I do? Those bits in soak, in the other trough?"

As Father John rolls up his sleeves, kilts up his habit, dons an apron, and sets about it, Father Bernard steeps in shame. He can well imagine their former abbot, Father Peregrine, involving himself in menial tasks around the place. But if he had, it would have been in conscious self-abasement, humbling himself to the way of service Christ had chosen, and showed those who loved him to follow. It would have been an intentional act of lowliness, to vanquish the stubborn pride of his aristocratic instincts. This man is different. Father John has scrubbed more sheets than he's eaten hot dinners, in the course of the years of loving service he's given in St Alcuin's infirmary. And the linens he washed there would, for the most part, have been fouler by a long way than anything dropped off routinely from the dorter. It occurs to Father Bernard that he has never once heard Father John complain – nor yet Brother Michael, their infirmarian now. They just got on with it, cheerfully and kindly; the service of their love, for the care of the old and sick.

When the job is done, they spread as many sheets as they have room for on the drying green, towels draped over the bushes of rosemary and lavender, whatever cannot be accommodated here hung on lines strung across the cloister garth, the washing prevented from drooping too low by forked props cut from saplings in the spinney above the burial ground.

"Back aching?" asks the abbot with a sympathetic grin, as Father Bernard straightens up. "Let me take the baskets back, then. I got there late, it's the least I can do. Then I think it'll be all about time for the midday Office. These'll dry nicely in this sunshine."

"Father John," says the sacristan. This is difficult, but he knows it should be said. "When you arrived, I'd been wrapped up in a very long internal monologue of bitter complaint. Thank you for coming to help me. It makes all the difference."

He feels the warmth of kindness and understanding, sees it in his abbot's face, those observant, evaluating eyes.

"Have you maybe been taking care of the laundry long enough, Father Bernard?" John asks him. "Is it time I asked someone else to pick this up? I think maybe you have enough to do with your other duties."

And Father Bernard starts to dismiss it, to protest that he doesn't mind. "Oh, don't you worry about me. I can fit it in. Today was an exception; there are usually two or three here to lend a hand. I'm used to it, Father. I –" Suddenly he stops. Why do this? Why pretend? His abbot is listening thoughtfully to his lies, his prevarications.

"D'you know," he admits, "I am fed up to the soles of my feet with this job. I've been doing it for years. There's no reason why I shouldn't – somebody's got to. But, a break from it… oh, dear heaven, what I wouldn't give!"

And his abbot is laughing at him, affectionately, understanding the way it feels. "I'll sort it out," he says. "Maybe Brother Richard, maybe Brother Giles. Let me give it some thought. I promise you faithfully, I won't forget!"

In the cloister garth, as Father Bernard watches his abbot pick up the laundry baskets to return, the warmth of the September sun brings out the fragrance of the herbs, of the roses Brother Fidelis trains up every inch of stone he can reach, knocking nails into the mortar for the twine that holds them up.

And it takes him by surprise, coming back to him as sharp and vivid as when he first came here, not much more than a lad: that this is a beautiful place.

Chapter Eight

As the sun climbs the heaven to its zenith, so the sound of the angelus bell ringing out from the abbey reminds the villagers to attend to their prayers; and then the brothers set their work aside for the noonday Office of Sext – the sixth hour of the day.

Living and dying, light and dark – they belong to one another, they cannot be picked apart. So it is that Christ who was called the Daystar, the Morning Star, was lifted up on the cross at the sixth hour of the day. As the burning sun tops the heaven, so he was monstrously and agonizingly exalted. And the tale is told that when at noontide they hammered in the nails and raised him high, there was darkness on the face of the earth.

"I am thirsty," Jesus groaned on his cross. And there was another noontide when the stories of Jesus tell that he was thirsty – the time he sat, tired, by the well at the edge of a Samaritan village, and begged a drink from a woman who came to draw water. He takes it gratefully, but he mystifies her when he says there is a way out of this cycle of weariness, toil, and aridity. There is a living fountain that springs up to eternal life. Nobody who drinks from this will ever be thirsty again. What? Where? The woman is bemused. But that's because she's used to looking outside herself for solutions. This one is hidden deep inside her heart.

So at the Office of Sext the community turns aside in the heat of the day to refresh themselves at the wellspring, to find the fountainhead that gives their life together whatever meaning it may have. They go back to the source. After they've done praying, a jug of ale won't go amiss, and the repast Brother Conradus has brought forth from his morning's labours. As Brother Walafrid remarked to Brother Giles only this morning, "It's not all holiness!" But Brother Giles capped that one. He lifted his head, with a puzzled frown, from his fragrant task of macerating herbs: "Yes, it is," he said. And he's right, of course; there's no getting round it.

Because man shall not live by bread alone, they have chapel first and eat afterwards. So Sext is not a sleepy Office, but sometimes the chant is augmented by the grumbling of stomachs.

Today, the first man into the chapel is Brother Paulinus. He's old, he's slow, so he set off early to make sure he wouldn't be late. He had to call by the lavatorium and give his hands a good scrub before he came into chapel. He managed to get most of the earth out from under his fingernails, but he's been podding the last of the beans today, before the haulm comes down. This afternoon he'll set them out to dry, so they have something to sow come next spring. All through the summer he's been picking beans and podding beans, and his fingers are all stained from the bean juice. His hands are clean, he's quite sure of it; they just don't look it.

He encountered Father Clement in the lavatorium, also making war on stains – but his are spectacular. He had an awful accident with a pot of red ink in the scriptorium this morning. By some miracle of divine intervention he can hardly believe even now, none of the manuscripts they were working on were damaged when he sent it flying. Because St Benedict's wisdom was the practical sort, they're all wearing black, so though three of them were well spattered, how can you tell? But between trying unsuccessfully to catch the pot when he knocked it, and muddling around attempting to mop up, he's got enough red ink on his hands to look as though he committed a massacre. He's upset. With every passing day some new thing happens to prevent him evading the insidious creep of his failing eyesight. He stands at the sink in the lavatorium rubbing uselessly at the gory crimson blotches. But it's no good. He'll just have to let it fade with time. He gives up and follows Paulinus into chapel, sits in his stall feeling miserable and old.

Brother Mark also comes to chapel via the lavatorium. His hands were sticky, because it's time to harvest the honey this month. The hive population is dropping, the drones disappearing – but he checked, and his queens are still there, though they are laying less and less. Time to replace them, though, now the autumn is coming.

Father Gilbert is already in chapel when these old men come in. He glances up from the music he's sorting in readiness for his practice this afternoon, and finishes the task as briskly as he can once he sees the community is beginning to gather for the Office.

Next in is Brother Peter, the ostler. He also goes to wash his hands first – and checks his shoes. He should really have changed into different ones for chapel, but he was in a bit of a hurry, so he didn't. After him comes Brother Fidelis, bent and rheumatic, walking slowly, smelling of the herb beds he's been weeding this morning. These days, if he tries to go quickly, he begins to wheeze badly and can't get his breath. It's a matter of taking things gently, he finds; accepting that the vigour of youth is gone. Provided he doesn't ask what his old body can no longer give, he can still accomplish most things in peace.

Their abbot enters the choir from the archway leading in from the ambulatory, and crosses to his stall. He marks the places in the breviary and psalter, then withdraws into himself like a closing sea anemone, hands tucked into the sleeves of his habit, cowl up over his head, eyes closed. The stillness in him makes you feel still, watching him.

The horarium brings a man into church seven times a day every day, and there is so much of the Bible that it must be pushed into every nook and crevice of time – at Collatio,[11] at mealtime readings, in private devotion, in Chapter, at Mass, not just in Divine Office. Understandable if at times he lets it all flow over his head, ceases to engage with the perpetual influx of Holy Writ and commentary thereon. The day breathes in the holy Word and breathes out prayer and praise, all the time, never stopping. The challenge is to keep it fresh, hold fast to the authentic and direct encounter with the *living* Christ, not some desiccated construct mistaken for deity, the accretions of dogma and doctrine, of dissertation and opinion, that sometimes posture as – but are not – the Holy Spirit himself.

The abbot sits in quietness, nothing in him moving but the patient tides of breath and blood, and the inscrutable arcane rhythms of the lumen of the gut. His heart settles over his community, as a mother hen fluffs out her feathers, lowering herself gently upon her brood, letting them creep in under her, finding her warmth. Deeper and deeper his spirit settles down, drawing this kindred of common life into his love, at the same time letting the light of his faith, his heart's yearning, expand into the infinite tenderness that bends over him, encloses him, adopts him.

Once he finds the still, small centre, the quiet home of prayer, he draws in after him the ways and wellbeing of Brother Cedd, pulls the heartache of his absence into the healing citadel of the innermost chamber of his heart. He does not move. His breathing is slow and quiet. He does not open his eyes. He holds Cedd there, where the lad belongs; with all the rest of them.

Brother Walafrid and Brother Giles arrive together. Today they are on the second stage of preparing tinctures for use in the infirmary – plantain and peppermint. They gathered them during

---

11 Gathering of the community for short, reflective reading before Compline.

the summer, a month or more back, and set them to steep. Now the mixture is seasoned, it's time to strain it through a fine-woven, double-folded cloth, ensuring the final brew is free of sediment and debris. Then it's sealed in the jars and taken to the infirmary. Today they've also found time to pound some herbs for a poultice to save Brother Michael the trouble – he has enough to do.

Father James, looking pleased with life, evidently in buoyant spirits, comes in behind them, and settles himself in his stall, opens the breviary, brings across the stitched-in ribbons to keep the page. He glances across at his abbot; then closes his eyes, peace on his face, recalled to stillness. His work has gone well today, flowed easily. The postulant seemed delighted with his robes, and with good reason – they were beautifully made and sat on him perfectly. It's been a good morning.

Father Francis, the prior, is next; his step as light and merry as the day he first came. Not much dims his naturally sanguine spirit – and people like him. Then Father Chad comes down from his library, his gentle, placid features thoughtfully composed. The almoner, Father Gerard, is there in good time. Like the infirmarian, the cook, the teachers, the cellarer, the porter, and the guest-master, he is often late or absent, for it's not always as easy as he'd like to detach himself from the lengthy histories and requirements of the needy. There are no guests at the present time – which is unusual – so Father Dominic is free to come to chapel, which is not always the case when they have a houseful. Brother Martin stays at the porter's lodge though, and says the midday Office quietly on his own.

Father Theodore and his novices – except Brother Cedd – all arrive in a group from their morning's lessons.

Brother Thaddeus takes a while washing clay off his hands, and comes into chapel when most of the community is already in place. Brother Richard is there, and Brother Cormac has locked up the checker and is sitting in his stall turning the pages of the big breviary, finding the place. Brother Stephen, along with Brother Josephus and Brother Placidus who have been helping him on the farm, slip in at the last minute, as Brother Basil finishes ringing the bell and loops back the rope. Father Bernard has been faffing about in the vestry, clearing up some incense he spilled when he was preparing the thurible for High Mass, but the silence alerts him to the imminent start of the Office and he hastens in.

Brother Damian isn't there – someone has to oversee the boys in the school through the day. They came into High Mass with him, of course, and he sat with them in the nave; but they don't attend the little hours of the Office. Brother Thomas is away until nightfall. Almost everyone who can be there is sitting with recollected composure in his stall.

As the abbot gives the knock and the community rises, Brother Michael slides into his place; nobody minds if Michael's late, you can't help it in the infirmary, they're just pleased to see him at all. But the last man in is Brother Conradus, cheerful and contented, arriving wreathed in the vague, encouragingly savoury aroma of some kind of stew.

The Office flows peacefully, as familiar to these men as the pulsing of their heart's blood through their arteries and veins. The opening prayer and humble presentation of their worship, the *Pater Noster* and the *Ave Maria*, the invocation, the versicle and response, the hymn, then the psalms of the day. After that the Little Chapter and short responsory, the prayer and the versicles and responses, finishing up with: *Fidélium ánimæ per misericórdiam Dei requiéscant in pace.*[12] Then one more *Pater Noster*, and Sext is accomplished.

---

12 May the souls of the faithful departed, through the mercy of God, rest in peace.

Chapter Nine

Brother Richard has never mastered the art of eating with his mouth shut. Perhaps it belongs more to the cultured refinement of the ruling classes. It's not so much that his mother never saw the need for so polished an accomplishment, more that her life had not encompassed the suggestion that anyone should try. Everybody eats with their mouth open, don't they? How else would they demonstrate adequate appreciation for the hearty fare slapped in front of them by their mothers?

Meals are taken in silence in a Benedictine monastery. This reaches beyond prohibition of speaking to the best diminishment they can achieve of clatter and scrape. None of this beating the dish like a gong as your spoon scoops up the last of the pottage. The only sound should be the voice of the reader – Brother Germanus this week – fulfilling the quota of scriptural material that will take them through the whole Bible in a year, and adding to it whatever edifying texts the precentor has identified as appropriate.

Every man among them has been schooled with utmost diligence by his novice master to be watchful for what is required – to pass the butter, the salt, the ale jug, when his brother has need of it. If a brother is lost in some reverie of his own, a discreet "ahem" may alert him that someone is waiting; or maybe he will suddenly feel his neighbour's foot covertly kicking his ankle. But his neighbour will not speak to him. They are in silence. If all else fails and the men adjacent prove relentlessly oblivious, there is the sign language of the silence, allowing an unobtrusive request to be made without disturbance.

As in the choir so in the frater – there is an order of seating. Father Francis sometimes thinks God must have it in for him, to have let it arise that he be allocated the place right next to Brother Richard. Self-contained, well-mannered, urbane, Francis considers his neighbour in everything, including the way he eats. In his own childhood, had he lapsed at table into habits like Brother Richard's – or not even habits, make that a momentary lapse – his stepmother would have removed his food without comment, and fed it to the dog. By the time he reached adulthood, an ingrained abhorrence of lip-smacking and slurping took root. Unshakeable. Inescapable. He just *hates* it.

Brother Richard is not entirely unaware of this. He doesn't realize of course that every time (in every meal of every passing day) that he breathes in his ale – and every spoonful of his pottage – with a long sucking slurp, the sound reverberates through every level of Francis's being in an agonizing intensity of irritation. It would be beyond him to imagine the extent to which it's possible for Francis to become focused in dread fascination on waiting for the inevitable smacking of the lips that accompanies approximately every third chomp of Richard's masticating jaws.

Granted, Richard is doing (as he thinks) valiantly. About twelve years ago, on a bad day, unable to contain himself, silence or no, Francis muttered in muted ferocity to his neighbour, "Oh, for mercy's sake, man! Can you not eat *quietly*?" This naturally drew Brother Richard's attention to the existence of a problem which he believes he has scrupulously corrected ever since. So Brother Richard, for twelve years feeling somewhat criticized and concerned not to offend, has excoriated Francis's soul at every meal they share. That's a long time. Francis has never mentioned it again. He feels ashamed that he ever said anything in the first place. Neither of them forgets. They carry the incident inside them, each of them, as part of the textured fabric of their relationship. There is no resentment. Francis wishes he hadn't given way to the grating on his nerves. Richard doesn't find it easy to sit next to a man so touchy you can drive him to distraction when you aren't even doing anything. From either side of an incomprehensible cultural divide, they each regard the mystery of the other. They continually patch the relationship with acts of kindness. In the absence of understanding, it's the best they can do.

There's nothing more Francis can say. There's no point in bringing it up with Richard, who would only be hurt and bewildered, or with his abbot, who could only laugh in sympathy and encourage him to be tolerant. This is what it means to take your way together.

In a fair world or a different abbey, Francis would have been gratefully rescued from this situation the day he agreed to take on the obedience of prior. He would have relocated from his place in the refectory to sit with other senior monks at the abbot's table. Unhappily for him, St Alcuin's is the monastery he belongs to. Their refectory is long and thin in shape. They do have an abbot's table, but there's only room for the abbot sitting at it, since, in order to make serving practical, the long tables where the brothers sit need to be a sensible distance forward from the walls. In a community with a keener investment in precedence, the monks might have been seated in an order determined by status. But not here. The senior monks sit nearer the abbot's table, true – but senior only in the sense that they entered first. The newer recruits end up nearer the door. Francis tries not to feel bitter about this circumstance born of the marriage of a leaning towards egalitarianism and a quirk of the architecture.

There are respites. Days when one or the other of them is serving or reading; the times – more frequent now Francis is prior – when he eats with the abbot in his house, or takes his place at the abbot's table when John has to be absent from the frater. But not today.

Brother Conradus, hampered by a steadily increasing reluctance in the cellarer to buy in any fish or fowl or cheese beyond what they produce themselves, has done what he can to produce an appetizing, beautifully seasoned meal of beans in gravy. It tastes good, but the sucking and guzzling of Richard consuming wet legumes makes Francis shudder. Nothing interrupts it but when he pauses to inhale some beer. The prior tries to be grateful that at least the man eats fast. Oh, no. He wants seconds.

Brother Germanus ploughs on with the careful dissection of biblical material in the set commentary, but the harmless flow of his reading is not sufficiently incisive to distract Francis from the sounds at his elbow that rack his tortured soul into spasms of revulsion. Quietly, outwardly unmoved, his eyes lowered, he eats his own food, trying to console himself with the reflection that at least, sitting right next to Brother Richard, he doesn't have to look at him.

The fruit is passed along. Francis chooses an apple, Richard takes three extremely ripe plums. It proves necessary to suck the disintegrating flesh from the stones and suck back the juice that escapes in quantities from his mouth. *Give him a huge tube*, thinks Francis. *Macerate the fruit, and just let him suck the whole lot up in one continuous gulp.* Then he reproaches himself for his sour and uncharitable attitude. He permits himself the indulgence of raising one elbow to the table as unobtrusively as he can, so his hand resting against the side of his face entirely obscures Richard from view.

Richard, replete, folds his napkin and tosses it down on the table with a cheery, playful air. He signals his satiation with a long, happy exhalation and a small burp. Then he occupies himself picking plum skin out of his teeth while he waits for everyone else to be ready. Francis sits motionless, his face disciplined into a pleasant half-smile.

The meal concluded, the abbot gives the sign and they rise from the long board. They clear their own pots as far as the table by the door. As the men filter through patiently, Francis and Colin reach the way out simultaneously. Instinctively courteous, Francis steps back, with a sketch of a bow and slight motion of his hand inviting Colin to pass. Richard, close behind, blunders into him and treads on his heel.

Francis is an affable, irenic soul, but if there's one thing that gets to him as surely as noisy eating, it's people standing too close to him – and he just hates it when someone treads on his heels. His endurance chafed to bleeding point already, annoyance flares inside him and he shuts his eyes. He quells the reaction instantly, hopes the postulant didn't see. But of course he saw. Every man sees everything in community. With the possible exception, perhaps, of his own annoying habits.

✠ ✠ ✠

Brother Tom stops in surprise. "Hello," he says to Brother Cedd. "What brought you here?"

For a moment, puzzled, his mind tries to make this fit; but no circumstance presents itself to account for his abbot having sent both of them to the same place on the same day without telling either of them the other one was going too.

Then, taking in how extremely nervous – even frightened – the young man looks, and since the abbot would hardly be sending one of their novices abroad in the world unaccompanied, Tom reaches the accurate conclusion that nobody has sent Brother Cedd here at all. He is not on abbey business.

"His feet brought him here. Sit down, Brother," says William, quietly; and they both do – Cedd subsiding anxiously onto his stool, Brother Tom with a smile of greeting in Madeleine's direction, releasing the scared lad from his gaze to give him a bit of space.

"This is welcome!" Tom comments cheerfully, adding, "Oh, thank you!" as William pours him a mug of ale. "Your brother sends his greetings, Madeleine – and the grain in those sacks is wheat in one, oats in the other. Left un-milled so it keeps better. Weevils always find flour somehow. Father John's given me permission to stay and make myself useful about the place so long as I'm back home for Compline. So I'm at your disposal."

Madeleine beams at him happily. "I cannot tell you how timely this is," she says. "The boots and the lovely warm clothes are a blessing, and the grains are a Godsend. But more than that, we are so grateful for your help. We've been busy picking apples and pears of course, but it does take a while to set them out carefully to store in the loft of the barn, so we've only picked as fast as we can pack away. William's been out helping our neighbours with their harvesting most days this month. They've a new baby, so the wife's lying in, which has left them shorthanded. We're glad to do what we can, naturally, but it's left me to gather and store most of our fruit myself – still, I've grumbled enough to make William wish he'd stayed home and helped me, of that I'm quite sure. Besides eaters and cookers, we do have quite a few cider apples, and I've a pile of those – along with the sweet apples that aren't good enough to store – ready for scratting in the cider press when I get the time to do it, or some help. And then William said the scythe needs a repair and sharpening, and there's a hole in the fence some beast has made, needs mending. So any help with any of that will be a blessing indeed.

"For myself, this afternoon I'm still picking the last of the beans. The haulm can come down next week; we'll be all done by then. Once all that's finished, one of us will have to go for some straw – both for bedding and thatching."

William, listening quietly, shakes his head at this. "I can't do the thatch, Madeleine, I've already told you. It's skilled work. We'll have to have some help with it. I think I'll need to hire a man."

Brother Tom detects the disciplined monastic humility in his tone, and thinks he looks a little overwhelmed. "I wish I could be here long enough to lend a hand with it," he says. "Still we – me and Brother Cedd, here – we can push on with the apples, or maybe I can fix the fence while he starts the pomace in the press? Whatever would be most help. This cheese is tasty, Madeleine, and I'm enjoying your bread, too. Warm from the oven. Couldn't be nicer!"

This time, he includes Brother Cedd in his glance as he looks across the table with a friendly grin; glad to see the young man fractionally relax. William sees it too, and very slightly nods as he meets Tom's gaze, warmth in his eyes. "Thank you, Brother Thomas," he says.

Tom directs his attention to the food in front of him, the fresh and fragrant bread, the golden butter still beaded with moisture, made today. There seems to be plenty of cheese, so he cuts another piece. "By heck, this goes down well! I don't know what's amiss with our supplies, but our cheese has been on shorter rations than usual these last few weeks. That'll not be Brother Conradus's doing if I know him – must be our new cellarer on a frugality drive. Mayhap you've been teaching him your ways."

William looks at him thoughtfully. "I wonder why that is, then? He's not had any advice from me about keeping men hungry. I drive a hard bargain, 'tis true, but I hope I'm not mean. Well, fill up here then – our cow came from St Alcuin's, it's the least we can do to let you have a bite of the cheese. Madeleine makes good ale and cider too, so drink up. And you, Brother Cedd – don't be shy; just take what you want, don't wait to be asked. We're honoured to have you drop by."

"What's most useful for me to put my hand to, then, Brother?" Tom asks, still chewing. Appreciation gleams in William's eyes; he treasures it that Tom thinks of him still as "brother".

"I think the handle of my scythe is past repair," he says. "I've bound it with twine, but it's still dodgy. I expect I could figure out how to remove it and make a new one, but if you think you're up to the task then I'll wager you'll make a better fist of it than I can. Would you be willing to take a look? Then maybe Cedd and I can take care of the apples."

"That shouldn't be too much trouble. Have you a lathe? Have you some seasoned bits of wood? Have you an anvil so I can peen the blade? Aye – good lad! You see – you're all set up! Taking to homesteading like a duck to water!"

Madeleine, observing her husband, takes note of the gratitude in his face as Tom says this. He has tried so hard and had so much to learn.

"Oh, we're all provided for," she says. "William takes good care of us, thinks of everything. It brings me peace, you know? I'm in good hands. He's a wise manager."

Her husband listens to this with a degree of astonishment, but thinks better of the humorous impulse to look behind him for some other man. Madeleine is not over-free with her compliments, and easily irritated.

"Thank you!" he says. "That's a plan, then. Well, if you're done eating, I'll show you where everything is."

Chapter Ten

Abbot John comes through into the kitchen when the midday meal is well concluded. He finds, as he hoped, Brother Conradus just finishing up. The servers have gone. Brother Richard has dealt with the ale and water jugs. The remnants of butter are scraped back into the big dish ready to take through to the dairy, and what is left of the bread is wrapped in big linen bags to eat later. There's never any leftover cheese to sort out. As much as he gives them, they eat.

"Thank you, Brother," says the abbot, "for another wonderful meal. It's a spiritual thing, your cooking. I don't believe I ever really thought about it before, but with the delicious food you prepare, you also serve up cheerfulness and wellbeing. You've improved the temper of the whole community. You've taken the level of contentment here up by several notches. I am so grateful."

Brother Conradus stands and listens to this, drying his hands on a blue and white cloth, his dark eyes shining with happy appreciation. He loves his abbot, loves the community, loves his work. Brother Conradus is a happy man.

"One thing," says the abbot cautiously: but in a monastic community the antennae are sensitive and receptive; tension enters the kitchener's body. Immediately anxious and on the alert, he waits to hear what his abbot has to say. What's he done wrong?

"That wonderful rice pudding you made us, Brother; it was so nice. The kind of thing I could go on eating all day. But I think – if I'm not mistaken – we had saffron in it. I'm just wondering if saffron isn't beyond the bounds of proper frugality."

He doesn't want to upset his kitchener. Lord knows what they'd do without him now. Men don't take kindly to criticism. But he knows he has to take this up.

To his relief, Brother Conradus's rosy, chubby face breaks into a big grin, his eyes dancing with delight.

"Saffron? Did you think so? Good! I wasn't quite sure if it would pass. Father, I wouldn't dream of using saffron; it costs an arm and a leg. Just every now and then we have some as a gift, and that's lovely, but I wouldn't ask Brother Cormac to get it in specially. Lady Agnes brought me some back from Cheppinge Walden when she'd been to Cambridge; it was superb, but it's all gone now. We used it for Hannah and Gervase, for their wedding feast. What we had in the rice pudding today was marigold petals. Brother Walafrid has been drying them for me. They don't taste the same of course, but to be honest it doesn't matter that much. The flavour of saffron is so delicate most people don't even know they've had it – which is a pity when it costs all that money. So I put honey and nutmeg in, and a little rosewater. The marigold petals serve to give it that lovely colour – and make people feel they've been given something special, which is always nice. I'm glad you enjoyed it."

The abbot gives silent thanks for this sensible, resourceful, creative man; that God sent him to no other abbey than this. It is a blessing.

"Thank you," he says. "I'm sorry to be so nit-picking."

"No, no!" Conradus shakes his head emphatically. "It's part of your oversight of us, Father. To see to it that we are frugal and responsible, that we live in humility and simplicity. It's part of your care of our souls."

John nods. "That's exactly right," he says. "But thank you for understanding. One other thing – I wonder, can I ask you to set aside two portions of something quite hearty? Brother Tom has gone on an errand for me today, and he may come in quite late; but you know him, he's bound to be hungry."

"With pleasure – yes, I'll put him something by. I'll see what I can do. We're a bit short on poultry and cheese just now, but there'll be bread aplenty and lots of fruit."

"Short on poultry and cheese?" says the abbot. "Why?"

"Oh..." Brother Conradus waves his hand vaguely in the monastic evasion John instantly recognizes as protecting someone else. "I think perhaps Brother Cormac felt we were getting through too much. I can be a bit lavish, overdo things at times."

The abbot frowns. "What? I don't think so. There's been nothing excessive."

"Oh... well..." He seems disinclined to pursue this, so John thinks he'd do better to leave it, take it up with Brother Cormac. "Anyway, Father, I'll be sure to look out something tasty and filling for Brother Thomas. I'll find something for him to enjoy. But two portions, you said. The other is for –?"

"For Brother Cedd." Before he can stop it, an entirely involuntary sigh escapes the abbot, and he sees in the kitchener's eyes that Brother Conradus has read the sadness stealing into his face. He wonders whether to say any more or not. Conradus waits respectfully, doesn't ask – knows he must not.

"I don't know if he will come back." John thinks this much he can say. "But if he does... I'd just like him to know we care about him. I'd like him to feel wanted – to know he's welcome."

Silence opens up between them like a pool. The helplessness of love that has no power to intervene, can only wait. Conradus understands.

"I'll be making bread this afternoon," he says. "And all the while I'm kneading the bread, I will pray for Brother Cedd. Our Lady – she lost Jesus, didn't she? She had to go back and look for him when he went missing. She looked for him everywhere, and when she found him, he was in the Father's house. This afternoon I will remind her about it. Our Lady is wise. She is good at looking for people who have lost their way. She doesn't give up. I will ask Our Lady."

There is such kindness in his voice, and with it such confidence, that John feels comforted. Perhaps, in the end, everything will be all right. He lingers, drawing strength from the steady, cheerful faith of his kitchener; but he has nothing more to discuss, and the silence is lengthening. Conradus probably has other things to do. So, "Thank you," he says, and turns to go. He takes in, without consciously noticing it, that Conradus's apron is clean. This soothes John's soul. The abbot believes in cleanliness. He doesn't know how it contributes to health, but he instinctively senses a link. His own standards of cleanliness for a kitchen apron varied a lot from Brother Cormac's. Brother Conradus washes everything – a world away from the perfunctory swipe with an already filthy towel Brother Cormac thought would do.

Between Conradus and Our Lady, the place is in good hands. If he thought about it, it would not surprise him to know that the first person Conradus commits into Christ's kindly keeping, as he watches his abbot go treading quietly out of the kitchen, is John himself.

"Ah, best of shepherds," the kitchener murmurs, as he finds the tape sewn onto the corner of the blue and white cloth, hanging it up tidily on the nail where it belongs, "you know what it is to feel the tug of loss when one sheep strays. Does not your heart follow after, wondering about brambles and ditches and vicious traps? Did you not break your heart for Judas, when he kissed you goodbye? Our Abbot John, dearest shepherd, he has gone through a lot this last year or two. Comfort his heart, give him faith and hope. Let him keep his flock entire. Bring this one home." He takes off his apron and hangs it on its hook behind the door. He casts a final glance round the kitchen, to make sure he has left nothing undone. Oh, yes. The birds.

On the table, apart from the bread saved for later, stands a bowl of scraps. These are not the ones for the midden, to rot down into good loam for the vegetable garden. In this bowl are a very few pared cheese rinds, some cut apple cores, apple skins pared away by the older brothers whose teeth are not so good, fragments of torn buttered bread left behind on the plates of one or two.

When Brother Cormac passed the care of the kitchen into Brother Conradus's hands, he didn't say much. Conradus, who is no fool, knew this did not result from indifference but from heartache. It cost Cormac dear, that act of obedience, turning away from the work where he felt at home, connected up to times past; especially since he was asked to shoulder, instead, the burden of a difficult area of responsibility. The work of the cellarer is tough and complicated, and Conradus doesn't envy him one bit. What Brother Cormac did say, that day he took off his filthy apron and tossed it with every appearance of utter carelessness into the laundry pile, was, "You won't forget to feed the birds, will you? They rely on it. And there are some mice underneath the woodpile. And the fox, he comes to the door at dusk."

Brother Conradus has his own opinions about feeding the mice, and was not astonished to discover how persistently they hang around the frater, despite the best efforts of the cat. No wonder, if Brother Cormac has been feeding them. Come inside, why not? Same man, nicer weather. He feels undecided about the fox. Will feeding it kitchen scraps save a few lives in the hen coop? Or simply encourage an extended family of hangers-on? He knew a householder who went in for hens in a big way, thought he would make a fortune selling eggs in the market, only to have thirteen foxes – thirteen! – move in, setting up house in a ring all around the farmstead. At a discreet distance. But not too far off, either. So Conradus has mixed feelings about feeding foxes. He remembers that.

He's willing to feed the birds though, trained as they are, by Brother Cormac over sixteen years, to expect the men in black to keep it coming. He carries the bowl out into the yard, where a hopeful Benedictine crow knows the hour of the day and sits waiting on the ridge of the small roof sheltering the well from falling birdlime.

Looking across at the watchful crow, chirruping to it in a friendly way as he broadcasts the scraps he's brought out, Conradus thinks of Jesus saying, "*Semper pauperes habetis vobiscum.*"[13]

Too true! A magpie lands on the jutting corner of the building, flicking its tail and scoping out the breadcrumb situation. Two sparrows come fluttering down, completely unafraid. No wonder. It would be entirely understandable if they mistook him and Cormac for their mothers.

Then a new thought enters his mind, surprising him. That thing Jesus said – "*semper pauperes habetis vobiscum me autem non semper habetis*" – the poor you will always have with you, but you will not always have me… he said it in response to his indignant disciples complaining about that woman who used up her expensive perfume anointing Christ's feet. They grumbled about it – jealous probably – and said she could have raised a lot of money to feed the poor if she'd sold it. So the point Jesus made was that some things were just for the everyday routine – but the chance to touch him was special and not to be missed. What Father Theodore, in Conradus's novitiate days, would have identified as the difference between *chronos* – time that is normal and just goes on and on – and *kairos*, the moment of opportunity that shines out from among all the other moments, saying "Now!" Though he treasures his full profession as a monk, Conradus misses those mornings in the teaching circle in the upstairs room with Father

---

13 "The poor you will always have with you" (Matthew 26:11).

Theodore. Even the difficult Greek, and learning new pieces of music.

But as to this business of having the poor always with you, but not always having Jesus, he thinks, it's tricky though, isn't it? Because, when it comes to the sheep and the goats – or Dives and Lazarus, for that matter – Jesus *identifies* himself with the poor! "*Quamdiu fecistis uni de his fratribus meis minimis mihi fecistis.*"[14] So, just as you might miss the *kairos* in the general muddle and jumble of the ongoing stream of *chronos*, you might overlook the Christ in the ever-present rabble of the insatiable poor. Because, when it comes down to it, perhaps it isn't as easy as you thought at first to tell the difference.

Here Brother Conradus pauses, checks himself, as his conscience intervenes with a footnote to the effect that "ever-present rabble" and "insatiable" betray a derogatory and disrespectful estimation of Christ's poor. For was not the Lord himself a poor man – poorer even than these birds, seeing they have their nests, but he had nowhere to lay his head. "*Mea culpa*," murmurs Conradus in penitence; then he hesitates. He's supposed to strike his breast, but he's got butter on his hand now, and doesn't want to transfer it to his scapular. He wishes he'd kept his apron on. He wonders if it will be all right to do it later, but knows he'll forget; so he strikes the air just adjacent to where his breast-bone lurks hidden beneath his robes and his own natural padding, and hopes that will do.

He stands to watch the birds chattering and squabbling over the scraps he's thrown, then takes the bowl back into the kitchen. He pours a little water into it, distressed at the bad job he makes of washing both his hands and the bowl, given that both are greasy and the water's cold. So he fetches the blue and white cloth, wiping the bowl and his hands and the water jug

---

14 "What you did for the least of these brothers of mine, you did for me" (Matthew 25:40).

handle free of butter. He goes to hang the cloth up again, decides his ways are getting perilously similar to Cormac's, and tosses it instead on the laundry pile, where his apron should have been too, by rights. Oh, bother it, the apron will do until the day ends; let it stay where it is just for now.

But what about the poor? And the birds? The fox? What about Brother Cedd? Is he, as it turns out, not the poor that will always be there, waiting for crumbs of love left over and flung his way, but the Christ himself, only briefly among them? Has he gone? Have they missed Jesus? Or is his soul still poor and hungry? Will he come back, begging for forgiveness, for understanding, for another chance?

Brother Conradus determines that if, in the trickling out of the day, the *chronos* flow of barely distinguishable moments, a sparkle of light picks out the *kairos* in amongst them, he will be ready. He walks along the cloister, thinking about it... the Benedictine crow, waiting humbly to be remembered... Brother Cormac begging him not to forget the wild birds who depend on them... his abbot, asking him to set aside a portion of something hearty... Christ's poor... Christ himself in humility among them... and Brother Cedd.

Chapter Eleven

Father Theodore waits. Though he holds his rosary loosely wound about his hand, his finger and thumb no longer isolate a bead to landmark his journey through the Joyful Mysteries. His murmuring of the holy words has ceased; but he hasn't stopped praying. His mind drifts, wondering, but all his searching unfurls within a consciousness of God watching over him, enfolding him. His reflections quest down into presence. Dumbly, blindly, he feels his way to the living water, not moving. His eyes are open, but now they do not see; he is reaching beyond the friendly confines of this familiar room – not outward; inward to where his heart is planted and derives its nourishment. He does not speak. His lips do not frame the shapes of customary intercession and invocation. Only his soul inches its urgent way to some kind of understanding. *Where is he? What's happening?*

He's waiting for Colin, but Cedd so occupies his mind that he doesn't even notice the postulant enter through the open door, presenting himself as the novice master asked him to, after the midday meal.

"Father Theodore?"

With a start, Theodore comes back to the present moment. "Colin! Your pardon – please – I was miles away. Do come and sit down."

It is only routine, this meeting, the novice master's care and oversight of someone new to the life, finding and feeling his way. Observing the young man now, Theodore can see too clearly the trust and admiration, the sense of privilege bordering on awe at this opportunity for private audience with his mentor. And Theodore – always – feels less than comfortable with this. What is he, after all? Only a man. What is his life beneath his best efforts at dignity and composure? The same struggle as everyone's, as Colin's own life. Scrupulously careful not to let his unease at being put on a pedestal manifest as evident irritation – for he knows how nervous that makes them – Theodore asks the usual questions, sits patiently with the usual silences and hesitant half-replies. Why is it like this? Why don't they have the sense to look ahead, to come prepared with whatever it is they need his help with, want to discuss with him? Why is it always like taming wild birds, shy and poised to take flight? He tightens his lips on a sigh that wants to escape. No.

But then, with time and gentle encouragement, the questions come. And Colin wants to admit his bafflement about obedience and permission. "I mean, what's the point?" As he takes heart, warming to his subject now, he lets the novice master see the frustration he's been feeling. "Every blessed thing! Humbly begging some vellum to write home on, a rag to wash the cloister floor, permission to get a drink of water for a cough or to leave our teaching circle to go to the reredorter – it's endless! So petty. Surely we can just be trusted to use our initiative? And the business of stopping *right now* – even if I've only that minute mixed some ink, or sized a letter and got the gold all ready. The bell starts to ring, and if I try to hurry, finish off, there'll be somebody's quiet voice saying 'Colin!' – and I have to leave it and start all over again later. What's so good about it? What's the point? Not to mention kissing the ground and confessing in Chapter every time I break a cup – even if it was already cracked – or lose my handkerchief. Or for the size and the gold I wasted because the

Office bell interrupted me and I had to start over. And bowing! All of us on our feet and bowing when the abbot comes along the cloister – and then having to follow him and kneel and confess if I didn't notice the first time! It –"

"Whoa! Whoa! Steady on! Can we try and untangle those things from each other? One at a time!"

Theodore unwinds his fingers from his rosary, rubs his eyes, thinking. "It does get a bit much," he agrees, "when you're new. And being in the right place at the right time – oh, that reminds me; you won't forget to go to Father Chad in the library at some point after None – and to Father Gilbert as soon as we've finished here, to practise the music for Mass and rehearse your readings?"

The young man nods. "I've remembered. And Father, I'm sorry I made such a pig's ear of the refectory reading yesterday. I went through it and through it, but…"

"It's the Latin," says Theodore, in quick sympathy, "along with being nervous. You'll get the hang of it. Don't worry about it. My fault. I should have realized you weren't ready for it. Still, never mind, it was only a first foray.

"So, then; what about this chafing obedience? Let's start with the matter of asking permission. I think of this as teaching us about community and responsibility. One of the main things we've given up is being able to say: 'This is mine.' Now nothing is mine. Having to ask every time is what reminds us. It recollects our minds to holy poverty. It makes us think about 'us' instead of 'me'. It teaches us a discipline of being responsible and accountable too. You know, we could get almighty comfortable living as we do – defended by stout walls, provided for. A roof over our heads, food for our bellies. We have our own farm, our gardens and orchards, our bees and dovecotes, money coming in from our desmesnes. Without humble obedience, seeking permission to use things and asking pardon for clumsiness and carelessness, without even noticing it we could drift from a common life of holy poverty to the complacency of corporate wealth. Expecting it all to be there for us, no strings, no consequences to our actions.

"As to the ink and the gold – well, there's the chance you wanted to use your initiative, surely? Pay attention to time passing, remember the wholeness of your day, the calling of your over-arching vocation. Remember that earthly things must be put aside, that there's a call and a context to your life. Otherwise, like some worldly people do, you'll get a shock when your time comes to die, lay it all aside however engrossed in it you are. Being alert, being watchful – it takes practice."

He looks, questioning, at the postulant. Reluctantly, not entirely convinced, Colin nods in acquiescence. So Theodore continues. "It's a renunciation of self-promotion and self-will, too. It fosters humility – all too beautiful at arm's length in other people, a lot less attractive when it comes home.

"And then, the bowing; well, that's humility too, in part. It teaches us what it's hard for every man to grasp – that I am not the epi-centre of the world. But as well as that, when I rise in acknowledgment of our abbot entering, and bow to him, for me it's saying 'thank you'. It's such a burden he carries, such a responsibility. Sometimes he gets so weary and so despondent – who wouldn't? I bow to his courage and faithfulness, to his willingness to serve us. I bow to say how grateful I am that I don't have to do it. Is that… does that help?"

Colin frowns. "You know what, Father? I'm not sure I really *think* like a monk yet. I see it but I don't see it, all at the same time. When you explain it like that I catch the vision, but when it comes to the daily application, it irritates like getting dust in my eyes."

Theodore smiles. "I'm sorry to disappoint you, but I ought to make one thing clear: it's not that monks think any differently or get used to it. It goes right on being like mud in your leeks. It's meant to. Humbling yourself, apologizing, giving way, speaking mildly, yielding your position – it's not even second nature, it's just *hard*. Only, it was what Jesus showed us to do because it's necessary for love. I tell you what makes it feel worthwhile – it's when you come to see that you're on the receiving end of it, too. When it dawns on you that the kindly welcome held out to you is not your brother's good luck in having a sunny nature, but him choosing to be gracious. Or when the ready forgiveness of some snide remark you made isn't because it didn't hurt him, but because he's passing up resentment in favour of forbearance. In the battle that rages over every human soul, he's got your back."

Colin considers this, turning the thoughts over in his mind. "Going back to what you said about obedience and having to ask permission," he says: "that it fosters community and responsibility. I can see the community bit, but how does it foster responsibility? Surely a man out in the world learns to be responsible because there's no one to help him – no one else to do it for him. Here, we just learn to do as we're told and leave the responsibility to our abbot."

When there is no immediate answer to this, Colin glances at his novice master, and it crosses his mind that today Father Theodore looks very tired and somehow sad. He feels worried in case his questions push too hard and seem impertinent or feel burdensome. He wonders if he ought to apologize, but Theodore says: "Cast your mind around the monastery. Let it travel. Think of Brother Michael in the infirmary. I know what he'll be doing today. Washing urine and excrement from men too old and ill to have control over their own bodies. Patiently feeding gruel to men who can no longer feed themselves. Washing their soiled sheets and bandages. Seeing to it that they get the right physic in the right doses at the right times so they aren't in pain or too chesty. Talking to them so they aren't lonely or afraid. Taking them outside to sit in the sunshine, tucking them round with blankets so they aren't cold. Checking supplies. Teaching Brother

Benedict the skills of nursing. But I wonder what he was doing last night? Was he at Nocturns – did you see? I didn't notice. Maybe he was sitting up all night long, keeping watch over someone near death, judging when to intervene, when to simply support someone's journey home with all gentleness. If that isn't responsibility, I don't know what is.

"Or you might like to think about Brother Cormac in the checker. If he gets the orders wrong, or doesn't keep up with market-place prices, or keeps slipshod records, the consequences will pass right along to the whole community – what repairs we can afford, who we can afford to employ, whether we have enough to eat, the standard of hospitality we can offer. Responsibility? I think so. The man in the checker decides what all of us eat.

"Or Brother Conradus in the kitchen, evaluating all the time how much to dole out and how much to spare, keeping the place clean and tidy, using his wonderful skills to see we have enough to fill our bellies and keep us in good heart, at the same time keeping faith with our commitment to simplicity and seeing we are not wasteful. Thinking about provision for guests and the abbot's table as well as the community. Planning ahead. Ensuring the meal gets to the table when the bell rings, even on days we're having hot bread. Managing to actually get to the Office himself! I'm glad I don't have to do it!

"I won't go on and on, I'm sure you get the point – but look: all these men live every day of their lives in obedience to their abbot. They surrender every skill and talent, all their strength and intelligence, to the community, in service of Christ. It's all laid down, nothing held back. And what's more it's to be done in cheerfulness, making light of it, saying 'this is nothing' when it feels like barrel-scraping, scoured-out, gut-wrenching, wrung-to-the-dregs *everything*!"

Something in the vehemence of this last gives Colin pause. He wonders how to reply. He cautiously explores the idea of trying simple truth. "Father," he says tentatively, "you sound very tired. Thank you. You've given me a great deal to think on. Would it be better I go? Would you like some quietness? And can I ask you – is it – er – are you feeling upset about Brother Cedd?"

This question, it seems, is not admissible. His novice master makes no reply. But Colin, observing the glitter of Father Theodore's eyes in the sombre mask of his face, the tightening line of his mouth, sees that it is so. And now he wonders about permission. He is supposed to wait until his master dismisses him. But maybe it's not always and only about rules. Father Theodore is, after all, only human. So after a few moments' hesitation, carefully not looking at his novice master, he gets up to go. After all, he thinks, when you live in community, solitude and privacy are the gifts of your brother's sensitivity. Sometimes it may be necessary to know when not to ask permission. How complicated.

Father Theodore says nothing. Colin, resisting the temptation to look back, quietly lets himself out. He seems to be learning more than he expected to today.

Chapter Twelve

Moments like this fill Colin's heart with wonder. He walks briskly along from the novitiate, scurrying down the night stairs to the cloister, the quickest route to the choir, through the south transept. Already as he strides the few short steps from the bottom of the stairs to the entrance of the massive church, he can hear the indistinct sound of singing. It rings out clearly as soon as he opens the door. Going in, he carefully and quietly closes the door behind him again, reflecting as he does so that he's already picking up on the mindfulness of monastic ways – and that makes him feel happy. Then for those few moments he just stands, listening, before he lets his feet take him, drifting, towards the nave where the spine-tingling sound carries like eddies and swirls of mist. And it is, he thinks, so beautiful.

The acoustics catch and swell the sound, bellying it out into an expanding cloud of music; just two voices – but how captivating, spell-binding. Before he came here, he didn't know music could be like this.

What he's listening to moves between the simple, peaceful river of plainchant and a complicated, cascading, bubbling, luminous effervescence of notes sparkling like light on a waterfall. What can it be? Whatever is this song they're singing?

And then the tissue of sound breaks into a few wobbly, misjudged notes, and collapses into the ordinary sound of Brother

Cassian and Brother Boniface laughing. The enchantment is broken, and Colin walks round under the gate in the rood screen to join the small group of men standing in the choir.

"Ah! Colin! You remembered. We were waiting for you – just running through the *Viderunt Omnes* – we shan't need it until Christmas of course, but there can be no harm in starting early. Especially because, depending on how you get on, we might consider attempting the Pérotin."

Colin looks at him. "The what?"

"Oh – I'm sorry. The *Viderunt Omnes* – the Pérotin setting is for four voices, where the Léonin we were singing is only for two. It's for the feast of the Circumcision, so we'll not need it until into Christmastide, but we have either option to fall back on depending how you get on."

"Father, I – I'm sorry to be obtuse – I don't even know what a Léonin is, or a Pérotin, or a vee... er – veed... er... what did you say?"

He feels so grateful that it's Brother Cassian and Brother Boniface standing listening to this, both of them grinning but entirely without condescension. He feels sure if Brother Felix had been part of the mix he would right now be shrivelling at the embarrassment of his ignorance. Father Gilbert doesn't sneer at him, though he doesn't think to conceal his surprise at this lack of familiarity with what, to him, is life and breath.

"Ah!" says the precentor: "I see what you mean. I do beg your pardon, I should have aimed for better clarity. What we were singing when you came in is the *Viderunt Omnes* – er, *Viderunt omnes fines terræ salutare Dei nostri*. It means, 'All the ends of the earth have seen the salvation of our God'. It's a gradual – you... you do know what a gradual is?"

"Oh, yes, of course I do! It's the hymn or the chant we have before the Gospel Alleluia."

"Yes, quite so. Now Léonin, working at Notre Dame –

that's in France – about a hundred and fifty years ago, began to develop some of these lovely descants and so forth that are trickling through to us now. And he worked with the chant, superimposing these top melodies that I think you must have heard our young men here singing. Pérotin came a little bit later – same place, of course – and built on Léonin's work. So his *Viderunt Omnes* is more complex – has the four voices against Léonin's two. And my great hope is that we may be able to tackle the Pérotin, with you on board. You – you can read music?"

"Doesn't matter if he can't," says Brother Cassian quickly, accurately interpreting Colin's expression. "He can sing the base chant, can't he? It goes so slow; just as long as he's got good wind and can do a tolerable imitation of a bull lowing, we can manage the rest."

Father Gilbert nods thoughtfully, not replying to this. "I can try," offers Colin. He thinks the precentor looks crestfallen, his eagerness punctured by Brother Cassian's prosaic take on the music in hand. "I'll do my best."

"Very good." The precentor pulls himself together and smiles at the helpful postulant. "Well, let's give it a go. I've got copies for the *Beata Viscera* here – that's also Pérotin. When you hear it, I'm sure you'll immediately recognize it because we sang it at High Mass just this last week when we celebrated the Birth of the Blessed Virgin Mary.

"If I explain the principle, and let these lads show you, perhaps it'll help you get a grip on it.

"With Pérotin, the tenor's the thing. He holds the melody – the chant. Now somewhere here" – he reaches over the ledge into the stall, muttering to himself as he roots about in the pile of scores to find what he's looking for – "Ah – yes – here it is. The *Benedicamus Domino* will serve as a perfectly good illustration. There are two treatments of it, two possible ways to go. Either the *discantus* – er, descant – or the *organum purum* – that's the florid organum, of course.

"Now look – do you see?" He indicates the place on the score and Colin, anxious to appear willing, peers at it cooperatively. "Syllabic chant melody, just a few ligatures – only the three, all simple. So that's our harmonic basis. What we do – look, you can see on the score – is stretch out the syllables, elongating the word, then superimpose the duplum, the new florid line that works towards the next note the tenor will sing. That's clear, yes?"

Just every now and then, in this new life he has undertaken, Colin has moments when he honestly wishes he was dead. This is one of them. He has absolutely no idea how to even begin to formulate a reply. He stands, his lips slightly parted, staring in complete blank bewilderment at Father Gilbert.

"Why don't we just show him?" suggests Brother Boniface good-naturedly, stretching out his hand for the music.

"Oh! Certainly!" Father Gilbert gives it to him, and roots about a second time to find a copy for Brother Cassian.

"Like this," says Boniface, giving Colin an encouraging grin.

Boniface takes a deep breath, then sets off in his clear, beautiful tenor voice: "Beeeeee – neeeeeee – diiiiiiiiiii – caaaaaaaa – muuuuuuus…" Brother Cassian gets ready, and as Boniface begins the "Dooooooo –" of *Domino*, he enters with a stream of notes like the music of a nightingale, this upper part continuing to ripple and flow above Boniface's tenor like a butterfly over flowers, the same glorious, transporting, free-flowing melodic waterfall as they were singing when he came into the church. They work through the syllables of the word together, Boniface slow and measured, Cassian creating the cascade of multiple notes. They both finally touch down on the same tone as Boniface reaches the last "oooooooo" of *Domino*. Then they all look at Colin.

"It's called a melisma," explains Brother Cassian.

"What is?" Colin loves it, but is beginning to feel too confused by the musical terms to even pretend to understand.

"Loads of notes allocated to each syllable of the text," says Cassian. His eyes, holding Colin's gaze, are full of merriment and kindness. "Don't worry," he says: "I'd never come across it either, but it's not as hard as it sounds. All it's made up of is one of us singing one word as long and slow and drawn out as you can possibly imagine, while the other one sings the same word, but all twiddly over the top. We both end up together. It's called 'polyphony'. It's how they do it in France. Father Gilbert's teaching us, so we don't get too stuck in the mud. We can be a bit behind the times up here in Yorkshire. He's making sure we're not."

"We – I expect you've seen this" – Father Gilbert looks at Colin hopefully – "I think Father Chad will have shown you – in the library we have copies of both Johannes de Garlandia's *De Mensurabili Musica* and Franco of Cologne's *Ars cantus mensurabilis*. I think you might find them very useful for your private reading – they explain the theory of the music most helpfully. Anyway – would you like to have a go?"

"Sing the base chant with me," says Brother Boniface. "Watch my hand; I'll conduct you through it so you know when to change syllable. *Benedicamus* again, Father? Off we go, then."

Colin has by now heard several such pieces at High Mass on Sundays and feast days, but this is the first time he's been invited to participate. The complicated explanations and unfamiliar terms make it seem so daunting that he doesn't even want to try, but the friendliness in the novices' faces encourages him, besides which he doesn't see how he could refuse. This is a requirement. So he stands with Boniface, and sings when he sings, through the long drawn out chanting of the words. Then Cassian once more fills in the complex, free upper voice. To his amazement, Colin discovers that it's all different when you actually join in. Just as chanting the psalms and responsories of the Office with the community lifts him above everything mundane to something peaceful and wholesome beyond imagining, so being part of this new polyphony is more exhilarating than he would ever have guessed. He feels his own voice, breath in his body, the power of his core, all the more intensely for the awareness of the other men's voices, uniting, blending. By the end of the two short words of the opening phrase, *Benedicamus Domino*, his eyes are shining.

Father Gilbert smiles. "Would you like to have a go at the *Beata Viscera*? We've got our four voices, and three of us are singing more or less the same thing at any one time. Don't worry if you go wrong. It's the only way to learn. Yes? You can sing with Brother Boniface again. It goes so slowly you won't have any trouble following your part on the page. Off you go, then, Brother Cassian – you have the opening verse as well as the top line."

Growing in confidence as they help him work with the unfamiliar forms, Colin feels excitement fizzing inside him at the discovery and the mastery of something so beautiful. Standing right inside the music, feeling the harmonies resonating through his own body, he is taken aback by how close it makes him feel to the men singing beside him; as though the harmony were not only musical but relational.

Father Gilbert looks happy when he sends the other two on their way, leaving some time before None to listen to Colin practise his readings. After a disastrous début the day before, intensive rehearsal seems like a good idea. Reading in refectory is a week-long job; it's only because Colin is very new that he had a one-off try at reading, to acclimatize him without overburdening him.

"I'm sorry I messed it up yesterday," he says ruefully. "It's so hard to read ahead and see what's coming. The Rule says only people who are good at reading should be allowed to, doesn't it? Maybe I won't ever be good enough."

"Oh, you will!" Father Gilbert sounds quite sure. "It's my responsibility to see to it that you are. Don't you worry about that. It's not next week, is it? It's the week after. So you can practise several times with me, and also when you're by yourself in your cell. You'll be magnificent."

The books themselves are large, meant for refectory reading, the lettering bold and clear. Someone – probably Father Gilbert – has already gone through the texts marking the stress syllables to assist with correct pronunciation, and here and there tiny margin notes have been added giving extra directions. Colin sees it's not going to be as difficult as he at first thought, provided he takes his time and makes certain to practise. Just now they're working through the book of Esther, which is an interesting story. This helps, because it engages his attention.

By the time the precentor decides they've done enough, reading in refectory has shrunk from being more terrifying than Colin can contemplate, to being a challenge he's not sure he can meet but wants to try.

"I think you liked the music," says Father Gilbert, as they carry the big reader's books back through the cloister to the recessed shelves under the reader's pulpit in the frater.

"It was wonderful," says Colin. "I loved it. What amazed me was how close it made me feel to the rest of you singing with me. I never expected that. It truly was harmony."

"Oh, yes," Father Gilbert agrees enthusiastically. "That's exactly right. Singing the Office, the Mass, every day – it creates the deepest bonds. And this is what's so exciting about the new music from France – the polyphony. It's community in music. Each man has his part to sing, but it has to be precisely fitted together with the other parts. It's a wonderful thing, as you said – it balances, varies, echoes, departs, and returns. It's how people are. And the key to it is, you have to sing loud enough for the man next to you to hear, and quiet enough so you can hear him. It's not for showing off or outdoing one another. The magic is in working together for the good of the whole. The world will see in time, you mark my words. Once they've got over grumbling about how strange and outlandish it is, they'll get the vision. People will see that polyphony builds community – it's the music of relationship, fellowship sublime."

Chapter Thirteen

Brother Conradus promised to pray for their missing novice, and he's as good as his word. He treads the cloister to the kitchen buildings with a most purposeful look in his eye.

Our Lady Queen of Heaven who watches over Father James working in the robing room is a being of indisputable glamour. Her mild and beautiful eyes, her rose-petal lips and creamy complexion, her towering crown and graceful fall of robes, combine into a heavenly sophistication beyond compare.

Our Lady of Good Counsel who watches over the kitchen is an entirely different perspective on the Mother of God. She stands on a table against the wall, near the scullery door. Our Lady herself is sometimes unsure whether the Good Counsel part of it is hers or Brother Conradus's, because he has a lot to say to her. He likes this statue. She's short and sturdy, with a capable look to her, holding the infant Jesus firmly; evidently not about to drop him or let him wriggle free. She has sensibly given him that lily to amuse him, since they will be here for a very long time. Her dress is a cheery red, and her veil faded blue. The baby Jesus in her arms has a lively, interested expression and sports a tunic in practical peasant russet. Nobody has splashed out on gold for this homely pair. Her nose is chipped, and one of her fingers has been knocked off. She was sent here from the chapel when Our Lady of Sorrows was donated. At her feet stands a pot, one of

Brother Robert's misshapes from his early days learning from Brother Thaddeus, with a casual posy of hawkbit, feverfew, tansy, and scabious, the last of the summer flowers, the ones Brother Conradus could still find to bring her.

"*Ave Maria, gratia plena, Dominus tecum,*" he murmurs as he fetches the flour and the yeast. "*Benedicta tu in mulieribus, et benedictus fructus ventris tui, Iesus.*" He goes for the jar of oil, and the precious salt. "*Sancta Maria, Mater Dei*" – he pauses before the statue, his head reverently bent – "*ora pro nobis pecatoribus, nunc et in hora mortis nostrae. Amen.*[15] Wait here. I'll be back."

He dashes into the garden to gather a big bunch of thyme – the best bread herb of all. Returning, he brings the fragrant bundle to the work-table, and begins expertly stripping the leaves from the tough stalks, into a small heap.

With a practised eye, he takes measures of flour, oil, and salt, and the mug of ale-barm[16] that Brother Walafrid brings over from the brewhouse and leaves out for him.

He dissolves a little honey in warm water – a jug of cold from the well, warmed up with a dipper of hot from the kettle hanging on chains over the fire. He mixes everything with the effortless familiarity of daily practice; and with the firm rhythm of kneading begins his prayer.

"*Ave Maria, gratia plena, Dominus tecum* – what are we going to do about Brother Cedd? He wasn't at chapel, Mother, and Father John is worried about him. Whatever does he think he's playing at? What's happened? *Benedicta tu in mulieribus, et benedictus fructus ventris tui, Iesus.* Blessed Mother, what do your eyes see? You searched for Jesus, your lad who wandered off; please search for ours now. You found Jesus where he said

---

15 The Hail Mary, prayer of the Catholic Church: "Hail Mary, full of grace, the Lord is with thee; blessed art thou amongst women, and blessed is the fruit of thy womb, Jesus. Holy Mary, Mother of God, pray for us sinners, now and at the hour of our death. Amen."
16 Froth skimmed from fermenting ale, used as leaven in the Middle Ages.

he was bound to be, in the temple, about the Father's work. Dearest Mother, search down your lad again. In the living temple of our lad Cedd's troubled heart, maybe your lad Jesus is fielding difficult questions again. *Sancta Maria, Mater Dei, ora pro nobis pecatoribus, nunc et in hora mortis nostrae. Amen.* Mother Mary, God trusted you with the care of his lad Jesus – for sure you can be trusted to look after ours. Now, look, Mother dearest, surely it's like this. If your lad Jesus is hiding in the temple of our lad Cedd's heart, well, if you go and hunt for him, search for him – your lad, I mean – look for him everywhere until you find him and bring him home, he'll have our Cedd attached to him, won't he, because that's where he'll be. So please… Mother, please… for me, for Father John, for Father Clement, God bless him, with his failing eyes… for Father Theodore – did you not notice, blessed Mother, he looks so sad today… for Cedd himself – he can do better than this… May it be so, dear Mother; may your lad Jesus find his way into our lad Cedd's troubled heart, and may you track him down right there and bring him home. Brother Cedd, I mean. With Jesus in the sanctuary of his heart. *Ave Maria, gratia plena, Dominus tecum…*"

Our Lady is well used to the fantastical confections of Brother Conradus's prayers. She can read between the lines. She gets the gist.

As he kneads the bread – stretching, pummelling, rhythmic – as he spreads oil on the lump of dough, covers it with a damp cloth, and sets it in a bowl to rise, all the while Brother Conradus does as he promised, holding before the blessed Mother of God, so fervently it cannot possibly escape the attention of her kindness, this lost sheep of the house of St Alcuin.

The plaster image is not the Mother of God. Of course it isn't; Brother Conradus grasps that for himself with no difficulty at all. He knows that all earthly things – even this place that he loves, even his own body, even the holy bread of the Eucharist and the beauty of the Yorkshire hills as they cup the light – are no more than what is passing and must be left behind. But he knows, too, that beyond and somehow within these familiarities of his life – the flour on his apron, the breath in his nostrils, the scent of woodsmoke, and the faded blue of Our Lady of Good Counsel's veil – lies the ineffable mystery of redeeming love. It is worked into his life as inextricably as ale-barm into his rising dough. And that's why he directs his prayers through a plaster statue. They are aimed at what she is, not what she isn't; not at a painted saint, but a love that never gives up on us, never abandons us, never turns its back.

He washes his hands. He takes off his apron and hangs it up tidily on the nail. "*Ave Maria*," he murmurs as the bell for None begins to ring, and he heads off along the cloister towards the chapel, "*gratia plena, Dominus tecum*..."

✠ ✠ ✠

The tinctures all done – cooled, strained, bottled, sealed – and Brother Michael's poultice herbs delivered to the infirmary, Brother Walafrid and Brother Giles start the next job. This week Brother Mark has taken the second harvest of honey, and brought them the wax to make a new lot of candles; very welcome – the cost of purchasing them would be steep indeed.

It's a slow process. They don't have so very much wax that they can heat it in a big trough, suspending the wicks from huge, rectangular paddles. The amount of wax would go down in the trough too early, leaving insufficient depth for the outer coats. So they content themselves with the two tall cylindrical pots they have, using a round dipping paddle that can take six wicks at a time. The wicks are made of braided linen threads – three, or more if the thread's unusually thin. Brother Giles cuts the resulting string to twice the length they want, plus an inch or so each side to allow for spacing and to attach the initial weights. Then he loops each length through two holes in the dipping paddle. They start with the church candles while the pot is full of wax, because those have to be tall. As the amount of wax in the pot goes down they use shorter lengths, making candles for men's cells and for the lanterns.

Every time they do this (*really* every time – Brother Giles has begun to find it more than tedious), Brother Walafrid comments on how much pleasanter and easier it is working with beeswax like this, instead of the tallow he had to make do with before he entered monastic life. Brother Giles could tell you, because he knows it all by heart, that when Brother Walafrid was a lad, for a start he had only wool to use for wicks, because that's what his mother used to spin; they didn't have any linen. And you had to let the tallow cool to just the right temperature with every dip, or the whole candle would slip straight off the wool as the layers built up, and you'd have to drop it back in the pot, let it melt, and begin all over again. Besides all that, of course it had to be rendered down with pot ash at least three times, and therefore strained through a cloth even more times than that, or it wouldn't harden sufficiently to set into anything you could use.

Oh, beeswax is a whole different proposition from tallow. It smells heavenly (as opposed to vile), it hardens fast, and adheres more evenly, which makes for a better burn.

Once the wicks are looped into the paddle, the little iron weights they keep for the purpose tied to the ends of each length, and the wax is fully melted, they begin the dipping. They have several paddles, and after every dipping they set each laden paddle into a rack with a drip-tray beneath, while it cools. Then they dip it again until the candles reach the dimension the monks want. At some point about halfway through, once the candles are heavy enough to hang down straight, they cut free the weights to prevent them being incorporated into the candles.

This is painstaking work, the more exacting because it does require vigilance – to get the work completed, the dips must be sufficiently frequent, but to get a good result, the thickening candles must be adequately hardened before each dip. That takes about a decade of the rosary.

The apertures for the linen thread in the dip paddles have slits extending from them clear through the edge, so each pair of candles can be eased off and hung as a pair over a rail when the job is done. This is the best way to store them; hanging there keeps them straight.

It's a hot job in a closed workshop on a warm day. The embers no more than glow beneath the grille on which the open pots of wax stand; even so, working in a room with a fire and several pots of hot wax brings out a fine sweat on a man in a woollen habit, even if he has got his sleeves rolled up and his skirts kilted as high as decency permits.

It's a pleasing piece of work, for all that; and nobody gazes more appreciatively on the tall, slender candles burning on the altar at Mass, or in the choir lanterns at Vespers and Compline, than Brother Giles and Brother Walafrid, who made them.

Chapter Fourteen

William sends Cedd in the direction of the orchard with the ladder, then turns back to the storeroom. Tom follows him in, looking appreciatively at the orderly arrangement of well-maintained tools and implements. He asks quietly, "Why has Brother Cedd come to you?"

William glances over his shoulder at him. "I haven't asked. He turned up here not long before you did. He looked agitated and distressed. I thought I'd feed him and give him a chance to calm down before I started my inquisition. I was hoping you might be able to shed some light on it yourself."

Tom takes the baskets, as William hands them to him, saying, "I'll bring the pitchfork as well as the rake. I think we might need them to pull down the high branches. I'd rather not shake the trees – it's a lazy way to carry on, it bruises the fruit. Don't worry, we'll find out what's gone awry with your novice before you have to go home. All being well you can take him back with you. But let's approach it gently."

They stroll down to the orchard, where Cedd is waiting for them, having carefully and sensibly set the ladder at a good angle from the tree, so positioned that it won't rock. The quick, appraising glances from both Tom and William do not escape him, and he sees they're satisfied.

"Do you want me to have a go at mending that scythe? One

ladder, one rake – this doesn't need three of us, does it?" Tom looks enquiringly at William.

"Aye – good sense. Are you all right to start up the tree, Brother Cedd? Shin up and I'll pass you a basket. There. Just give me a moment while I show Brother Thomas where I keep the things he'll need – I'll be back before you know it."

Once they have two big baskets of apples, William suggests they take them up to set out in the loft. "If we tumble them out here, they'll bruise, they'll pick up insects. Let's take them straight up and start again. A bit laborious – I'm sorry. My fault – we should have more than two baskets. But generally it's just me or Madeleine, and it seems enough."

They climb up into the spacious loft over the barn, filled with shelving to store the fruit through the winter. Trays slide out of the racks to fill with apples. "Over here," says William. "These are good keepers. We have to store like with like or we'll get in a muddle. You know not to let them touch one another? Of course you do. The aroma of the apples up here is wonderful, don't you think?"

Then, as they place the fruit with care onto the racks, William asks casually, "Why have you come to us here, Brother Cedd? Did you want my help?"

The novice doesn't answer immediately. William waits. He can sense – smell – the boy's nervousness.

"If I'm honest…" He stops. William says nothing. He knows being honest sometimes has to travel up from a very deep place. "It was… there were… I thought you would understand, because more than once while you were with us at St Alcuin's, across the choir I saw you sitting with your eyes closed, tears rolling down your face."

William digests this information. "Aye," he says drily, feeling the lad hoping for some encouragement. "You probably did. As to understanding, you can try me. I'm not renowned for sympathy, neither for kindness. But I'm willing to listen. What's the trouble?"

"Well…" (*Look what you're doing with those apples*, William thinks, but he says nothing.) "I so desperately want to be a monk. Since I was a child, it's all I've dreamed of – all I've thought of. To lead a holy life. To please God. And St Alcuin's is everything I imagined, everything I wanted. It should be a dream come true. But I suppose I never put the two together – the place and me. I knew what I wanted, and I used to come up to the abbey to Mass sometimes; so I watched the brothers and I talked to some of them. They're much as I expected. But I feel… so awful."

William has finished setting out the apples in his basket. He takes Cedd's basket out of his unresisting hands and continues with those. "Because?" he says.

"Oh, basically, I'm so stupid. I don't know much and I'm not clever. I'm not very quick to catch on and I'm not witty. I don't pick up hints – I'm slow to notice when somebody needs something passing or doing. I'm not popular; I have no accomplishments and I can't make people laugh."

No, I can imagine, thinks William as he listens to the pathos in the young man's dismal tone. Having finished setting out the apples he places the baskets by the hatch in the floor. He leans against the crossbeam, his arms folded.

"Have you heard of Francis of Assisi?" he asks. "Italy. The preacher. Started an order of mendicant friars."

"Yes." Brother Cedd nods, though he doesn't look very interested. His thoughts are turned inward.

"Well, according to Francis, we must bear patiently not being good and not being thought good. I think that's how a holy man says, 'Grow up and get used to it.'"

Cedd raises his bent head to look at William. He looks close to tears, and beneath the physical exterior, William sees the lad's soul flinch. Something in the novice's face reminds him of himself a very long time ago, needing refuge and compassion, finding neither.

"I'm sorry," he says. "I told you sympathy isn't my strong point. So... forgive me, I still don't really see what the problem is. You wanted to be a monk, now you are; the community is all you hoped. You're neither a scholar nor a wit, but no one's complained. So...?"

"I feel such a failure," the boy whispers, wretched. "I have nothing to offer, no contribution to make. I can't make any kind of difference. I might as well not be alive – in all truth, I'm not really sure why I am. I feel so disappointed in myself."

"Insignificant?" says William, and the lad nods. "Unexceptional?" And he nods again.

"That'll save you a lifetime's struggle and anguish, then; because that's what you're meant to be. *Humilis* – lowly and humble and of no account. Now, if you were a gifted poet or theologian, if you were everybody's darling and overflowing with talent, think how hard it would be to achieve humility."

Somehow, this isn't going as Brother Cedd imagined. "I do know that it's good to be humble," he says: "that I should seek the lowest place." (*Perhaps you've found it*, thinks William, but decides the novice wouldn't find that funny.) "But even so, I still want... still need –"

"Constant reassurance? Aye, don't we all."

Brother Cedd looks hurt. "It's not that I want to be special," he protests, but William comes back at him: "No? Are you sure? Then what's the problem?"

"I feel so full of shame at the person I am. Such a failure. And I thought you'd understand."

"Thanks!" says William, realizing too late that there is no point of entry corresponding to his sardonic sense of humour in this young man's soul. "I'm sorry," he says. "That was meant to make you laugh. Never mind. All right, here it is, then. For sure

I understand. I know exactly what it feels like to be a nobody, an object of disdain. I know what incompetence feels like and I have a lifetime's experience of shame. When I said about Friar Francis, it's because his words comforted me, struck a chord with me, since I know all about not being good and not being thought good, and bearing it patiently, because what other options are there? Brother Cedd – friend – that's just life. It's mostly a matter of sawing logs and chopping kindling, fetching water and stirring porridge, mowing grass and spinning wool and kneading dough, mending fences and clearing ditches, cooking meals, eating them and washing up. You have to find something beautiful in it or you'll go crazy. I think being starved and incessantly abused and beaten when I was a child helped me see those things in a cheerier light. They look less dreary and mundane when they represent safe haven, some kind of refuge from the storm. Maybe – perhaps you just have to stop worrying about how you're doing, and get on with life? They let you join, they let you stay; that might have to be enough.

"I do wonder, though... your novice master – I'll wager he's said to you at some point, if you think something's missing from the community, see if you can put it there yourself."

He lifts his eyebrows enquiringly, and Brother Cedd affirms it. "Yes. Father Theodore often says that."

"So – could you try that? Seems to me what you're hungry for is someone to say 'Well done, lad. That was a good idea, that was a nice piece of work, that was sung well, you're doing grand.' Yes?"

"You make me sound self-absorbed and childish," mutters the novice.

Aye, you are, thinks William, but he continues: "Might you assume other people feel exactly the same? Might you take on the task of putting into the community the affirmation and reassurance you wish was there? And could that become your contribution?"

This is greeted with silence. Then, "I wasn't sure I'd be going back," mumbles Brother Cedd. "And even if I wanted to, they might not want me now."

"What? Didn't you just tell me, the thing you always longed for was the life of a monk? Why would you not go back? As to *them* wanting *you*, so far as I can tell, you're missing something. This life you've embarked on – it's not about you, nor even about the community. If you think it's either of those you'll be disappointed every day of your life, because living up to expectations is what no human ever has done since God made Adam. The point of a holy life – well, no, forget about being holy – the point of *any* life is to encounter Jesus Christ, to walk with him as a friend, to open your heart up for him to dwell in. You... you just ask him."

The novice looks at him, curious, at a loss. "What do you mean?" he says.

"You ask. You speak to him – to Jesus. To heal your soul, to bring his peace and healing. To do whatever he wants really; just to come to you. If you want that, you have to ask."

Brother Cedd looks intrigued and puzzled. "Speak directly to him, you mean? To Jesus? Not a canticle of praise, but like I'm speaking to you?"

"Aye. That's exactly what I mean."

Cedd turns this unfamiliar proposition over in silence. Then, "It sounds as if it should be something quite ordinary, a little thing, the way you put it," he says: "but when I think about it, I feel shy to do it. Can you – will you ask him for me?"

"*Me*? No! I think – it's a thing you have to do for yourself."

"But I don't know how to. I don't know the words you have to say. I don't know the prayer."

"No – look, Cedd – you're not getting the hang of this. You have it all wrong. Perhaps I didn't explain it properly. This thing, well, there's no liturgy for it. It isn't a formula. It's just straightforward – you just make your heart open, and invite him in. And then you walk with him. It's not about saying prayers – not even if you're a monk and you have to be in chapel seven times a day – it's about a life that prays. I don't know – maybe like a daisy open to the sun, turned towards the light. No, sorry, that's not very good; I don't suppose you aspire to be like a daisy. Anyway, you just do it. That's all there is to it."

"And you think, if I ask him, if I invite him like you said, he'll help me not to feel such a failure – not to feel so worthless and ashamed?"

William hesitates. Life, he knows, can be as littered with hollow promises and shattered dreams as a garden, where blackbirds and missel thrushes nest, is littered with empty snail shells. A graveyard of sorts.

"I have no idea what he'll do," he says. "He's not at my beck and call."

"But... *would* you do it for me?" the lad begs. "Would you say the prayer? And I'll say *Amen* at the end."

To the depths of his soul William wishes he hadn't got into this. The prospect of making so intimate and personal a prayer – aloud – in the presence of another, makes him squirm. *Say your own blessed prayers.* Right now, he thinks he might actually hate this boy. But, "All right," he says. Without giving himself further time to think, without kneeling or straightening up from slouching against the wall, without even unfolding his arms, he shuts his eyes.

"Lord Jesus," he says softly, humbly. The tenderness in his voice takes the novice by surprise. He thinks this is how a man might speak to the person he loves best in the world.

"Brother Cedd here, your lad; he needs to know your love for himself. He needs to find you and follow you. So much confusion and discouragement, so much disappointment. Failure and broken dreams. It's painful, my Lord. It hurts. All of us want to be worth something. Look, Lord Jesus, here where he opens his heart to you. Please come in. Please forgive him for everything that's offended you. Oh, my Lord Christ, I beg you to have mercy. It clags up inside us harder and harder – the fear and resentment, the peevish complaining, the comparisons with other people, obsession with self. Sulkiness and petulance and self-pity. Have mercy, oh have mercy. Dissolve it away until your love flows free inside him, flows like rivers. Come to him, Lord Christ, with all that hope and joy. Give him your peace, like you promised. Give him grace to start anew. May he – by the miracle of your love for him – may he be born anew."

Brother Cedd is still coming to terms with this assessment of his character and diagnosis of his problems, taken aback and more than slightly offended, when William says: "Amen."

And the novice thinks: *What's to lose? Why not?* He's so tired of the way life is. It couldn't get much worse.

Still with his eyes closed, without moving, William says: "'*Venite ad me omnes qui laboratis et onerati estis et ego reficiam vos.*'"[17] And Brother Cedd says: "Amen."

The silence intensifies into presence, personality. Neither one of them moves. Then William opens his eyes and he looks at Cedd, and he knows. He nods, seeing it. Then, apprehending the rising tide of emotion, afraid the boy might be about to gush or – even worse – try and thank him: "I think we're shirking our chores," he says. "Shall we go and get some more apples?"

---

17 "Come unto me, all ye that labour and are heavy laden, and I will give you rest" (Matthew 11:28 KJV).

Chapter Fifteen

The Office of None is so called because it marks the ninth hour of the day. At this hour, Peter and John went up to the temple to pray and healed the man begging at Beautiful Gate,[18] Cornelius the centurion had his vision,[19] and Jesus died. Those things happened a long time ago, but the great cry of Jesus, "It is finished!", is carried in the heart of every brother every day, for that accomplishment directly affects them, being the work of their salvation.

Momentous as the death of Jesus surely is, and though monasticism perseveres with the psalmist's "seven times a day do I praise Thee", there's no doubt about it: the Office of None obtrudes annoyingly into the day. So Brother Stephen thinks, anyway. In the summer timetable, because daybreak is so early, he nips up to the farm after Lauds and breakfast to milk the cows. If he's quick and has help, he can get the cows milked and turn them out to pasture before Prime, first Mass, and Chapter. That means legging it up the hill and setting about it with dispatch – but what else can he do? A cow needs milking. Everything else gets left, and even then he's often late for the Office, sometimes even late into Mass. If there's any serious business dragging out the Chapter meeting he has his work cut out, because after that

---

18 Acts 3
19 Acts 10

it's back up the hill to strain the milk, feed the pigs, and look over the sheep. He swills down the house where the cows are milked and the dairy, but in truth it's often a hasty job, because through the morning the novices are at their lessons and he has no help. The poultry aren't his job; Brother Giles looks after them.

He barrows the milk down the hill to the kitchen, has a quick wash, and goes in to Terce and High Mass. Then back up to the farm to attend to whatever work awaits him until the bell rings out for Sext and the midday meal.

After they've eaten, he can have one or two novices, sometimes a few schoolboys if their lessons are done for the day, even Brother Giles and Brother Walafrid (though not today) to help him around the farm. In these last few weeks he's scavenged all the help on offer to get the fruit in and the grain, glad of a stretch of fine weather after so many wet summers.

But what really tries his patience – whether they're cutting rye, barley, oats, wheat, building the ricks, mending a wall, whatever they're working on – is having to come back down for None smack dab in the middle of the afternoon. None takes barely more than a quarter hour, and it drives him mad when they must every man of them down tools, walk all the way along the farm track and all the way back up again after, for a few psalms, a couple of Bible readings, a canticle, and intercessions for the world's poor and struggling. What makes him feel even worse is his deep, inescapable shame at regarding the Divine Office as a tedious interruption to necessary farm work. When he needs no one to tell him, what he came here to do is hold all life, including his own, before the loving face of Almighty God, and make of his hours a ceaseless stream of thanksgiving, praise, and prayer. The rest he manages to juggle with good grace. It's None that gets him.

Just now he's refusing to look ahead beyond Michaelmas when they change to the winter hours. The days will be shorter, beasts out to pasture in the summer will be in the byre and needing food fetching for them, and the shrinking days mean shorter intervals between the obligations of the monastic horarium.

From Lammas right through to last week, as many brothers as the house could spare have laboured to bring in the grain; it's all safely gathered in. So today, Brother Stephen, with Brother Placidus and Brother Josephus to help him, has been threshing, winnowing, and sieving wheat up in the big barn. He's pleased; they've done well. When they hear the bell begin to ring for the Office, obediently they set aside the flails, unroll their sleeves, and unkilt the skirts of their habits, shaking out as much as they can of the dust and chaff, rubbing it free from their hair, knocking it out of their sandals. Then they set off at a good pace down the hill to the chapel.

Brother Stephen asked his abbot's permission to work through the afternoon during harvest. At the height of it, in mid-August, seeing the weather was holding and the whole community depends on that grain for the winter, Abbot John agreed to it. But now the sheaves are in under cover, he insists Stephen come down every day for None. "It's what you're here for, Brother," he said. "I know how vital your work is on the farm – it was the same for me with the infirmary. There was nothing that could be neglected or put to one side. I was responsible for the wellbeing of sick men, as you have the care of livestock and the task of feeding us all. It is no small thing. But – or so I often thought when it exasperated me to stop right in the middle of something to be present with the community at prayer – there's a snare in this. Because the work is essential and won't wait, the temptation is to begin to see the duty of prayer as a lesser thing. As something small and distracting, an addendum to what really matters. I can't tell you how often I had to admit that line of thought to my confessor. It's a dangerous track to follow: that way travel the lost.

"Whether or not someone is dying or a ewe is giving birth, the work of prayer is still our central calling and our first duty. So, no,

I'm very sorry; you do have to come down the hill and join us for None. What you are is a monk, not a farmer."

Brother Stephen heard this in silence. Sometimes when a man does not speak, it's a form of resistance: a refusal to engage. Not in this case, and his abbot did not mistake Stephen's silence for obstinacy. He stood, mulling over what John had said to him, and eventually he replied, "Aye, you're right. Please forgive me. I got carried away. Father Lucanus – your novice master too, wasn't he? Or did you have Father Matthew? Anyway, he used to say to us, 'Be wary, lads, watch yourselves. Have a care not to get possessive, not to get wrapped up in the work you do. Keep one step back. Remember you have only one job to do, and one Master to serve. Leave the men of the world to fall in love with their occupations if they find it satisfying. You keep your eyes on Jesus.' Comes back as if it was only yesterday. That's what he used to say. Drummed it into us at every passing opportunity. And look at me – I still forget. I'm so sorry."

His abbot's eyes shone with affection and respect. "Thank you for understanding," he said. "And when there's something you simply cannot leave, well, I will understand too."

And this afternoon, just as Brother Basil stops ringing the bell, Brother Stephen, Brother Placidus, and Brother Josephus, fragrant with the dusty goodness of golden grain, are in their places in the nick of time before the abbot gives the knock and the community rises to pray.

✠ ✠ ✠

Not everyone experiences None as a maddening interruption of vital work. To some men sometimes, this brief space of prayer and chanting feels as though you just threw them a lifeline. As it does to Brother Damian today.

This all begins earlier in the day when he says he can manage without Brother Josephus in the abbey school, since Brother Stephen is looking desperate about extra hands still needed up on the farm. Normally Brother Tom will help out until the grain is all threshed and stored, but the abbot has sent him off on some errand that will fill up the entire day. Colin is handy and practical, but Father Theodore says they can't have him today because Father Gilbert needs him to practise his singing and his refectory readings. When Brother Josephus says he'll go up to the farm then (reluctantly), neither he nor Brother Damian realize that Father Gilbert wants two of the novices as well as Colin, and one of those is Brother Cassian, which leaves Brother Damian on his own in the school.

The boys are in boisterous spirits, having spent most of the last three weeks picking fruit and generally larking about on the farm. Brother Damian is put to it to get them even sitting still and paying attention. One particularly over-excitable juvenile, given to pinching his neighbour and causing much hilarity among his classmates by finding it necessary to fall off the bench, or drop his stylus, or sneeze explosively, or shriek when the boy next to him pinches him back, eventually exhausts Brother Damian's patience.

Attempting nothing more taxing than teaching them, line by line, the Apostles' Creed, he finds the task made untenable by this delinquent's relentless and asinine interruptions. And in the end he loses his temper.

"Ah! Damn it, child!" he blazes at him. "Whatever devil of hell took up lodging in your brainless skull? Are you out of your right mind or didn't anyone ever teach you how to behave? Were you dragged up in a barn, you confounded little wretch? Can you not sit still for two minutes together? One more word from you – I mean it; *one* more word, and by the Mass you'd better believe it – and I'll have that birch down and really give you something to squawk about!"

Now, this threat quickly proves unfortunate. Consumed with

gruesome childish eagerness to see one of their company tortured, from this point on the rest of the class spare no effort to goad the lad in every imaginable manner. Every time Brother Damian turns his back, or even takes his eyes off the boy, someone tweaks the lad's clothes or tugs his hair or pulls a mocking face at him. Not a placid individual at the best of times, he's beside himself under this concentrated torment – all of it covert, sly, and most artfully concealed from their infuriated schoolmaster. Twizzling and thwacking, exclaiming incontinently, for no good reason that the master can see, the young scamp generates such mayhem that in the end Damian is ready to make good on his word.

His face grim, he dismisses the school early. He does what he can to redeem things from an appearance of disintegrating out of control, by telling them Brother Stephen has so much work in hand he has no time to forage for morsels to feed the pigs. This is entirely true, of course – always – though it omits the detail that, seeing pigs are ideally adapted to foraging for themselves with no help from anyone, searching out delicacies to tempt them is not how Brother Stephen would have spent any afternoon. But Brother Damian tells them to find a pail up on the farm for whatever they collect – be it beechmast, acorns, toadstools, slugs or snails. "And don't bring them back here," he thinks to add: "I don't want them. The pigs'll be in the orchard like as not – you can take them up there. Once you've fed them, you can go home."

Collaring his young ruffian firmly when the wretch hastens to escape through the door with the others, who look back over their shoulders grinning and pointing as they set off, Damian keeps a relentless hold on him until they've gone. He pushes the door shut after them with his foot, and drags the now frightened child across the room. He feels the boy's panic and the turbulence of his fear, but he doesn't care because he's angry. Grim with rage, he tightens his grip on the resisting, protesting boy and grabs the birch down from its nail on the wall. There's no likelihood of the child keeping still, that's not his temperament, nor is there anything calm and measured about this; it's a fight to hold him. He's too big to go over Brother Damian's knee, but the monk, capable and strong, roars at him to shut up, slams him face down onto the master's table, and pins him there with one hand firmly planted on his back. Irate, he slaps the birch down alongside on the table to get back a free hand for roughly yanking down the boy's breeches, then grabs the rods and gives it all he's got, six vicious stripes before he lets him go. Furious as he is, the sight of the lad's howling red face running with tears as the boy struggles his clothes back in place, gives him immense satisfaction. The birch hurts. He knows it does. He left red, swelling weals where he sliced him.

"Now get out and don't come back here until you can behave!" he yells at him. Still bellowing, the child turns and runs, knocking a bench over as he stumbles into it, yanking the door open so that it crashes back against the wall as he goes.

Alone in the classroom, still angry, Damian hangs the birch back up on the wall. His heart hammering, he sets about tidying the room, restoring order. He picks up the kicked over bench, straightens all the benches back as they should be, collects the boxwood wax tablets that have dropped to the floor in the eager exodus, kneeling down to retrieve styluses scattered here and there. As his rage subsides he feels shaky and upset, but he doesn't want to acknowledge it. The child behaved abominably. He deserved a thrashing.

Eventually the room stands in impeccable condition. There's nothing left to do. And Damian feels rotten. He pulls the door shut behind him as he leaves the building, and walks, his shoulders hunched, looking at nothing but the dust of the ground, to the church. He takes refuge in his stall and, within the shortest time, Brother Basil begins to ring the bell for None.

Force of habit has Brother Damian sitting, standing, uttering responses, saying his Amen; but his mind is in turmoil. He tries to find a way in to the peace and cannot. He can hear the child bawling, see the tears, see the rising red stripes on his flesh. Even so, the serenity of the Gregorian chant gives him something to hang on to, a means of re-establishing some kind of core.

At the end of the Office, as the brothers go about whatever the rest of the day contains for them, Damian reverences the presence of Christ in the sanctuary and turns to go, but listlessly now.

Brother Cassian appears at his side. They shouldn't talk in church, but, "Are you all right? School went smoothly?"

Damian just looks at him. "No. I think I'd better talk to Father John."

He turns back, and there is his abbot, eyebrows raised in enquiry. Cassian sees where he is not wanted and discreetly withdraws.

Brother Damian walks back with his superior to the abbot's house, and John listens seriously and attentively as the young monk tells him what happened. "When you say you hit him hard," he asks, "what do you mean? Did you break his skin? How many times did you hit him?"

"I gave him six strokes with the birch, which is more than he deserved, and I didn't hold back. Not enough to cut him, but... I was just out of my depth," Damian answers. "And I'm sorry, Father. I'm so sorry. I'm so ashamed of myself. I should have been able to do better than that. It was... violent. Horrible. Such a skinny little runt – nothing much of him; and me a grown man. I should be taking responsibility for the situation, not thrashing him with sticks."

Boys are beaten every day, of course, and expect no sympathy from their parents and teachers. It's just the way of the world. But he wonders: "Does it mess things up even more if I apologize to him? He was badly out of order, but if I'm honest, so was I. It got past a reprimand or a just punishment. I scared him, and I really hurt him. Can you – I was too rough with him, Father. I frightened him. I… well… can you – should you – say sorry to a child?"

The abbot considers this in silence. He thinks of his bishop, who at the last visitation chided him for letting the birch gather dust, told him it must be laid on harder and more frequently. He thinks about that, and about the accustomed ways of keeping discipline in school.

"I don't see why not," he says. "It's hard to move on from something you regret if you don't put it right first. It lodges inside you. And I'd rather the lads in our school learned from us that power is meant for gentleness. Think carefully, though. You can't back down from your authority or your requirements of him, or you'll mire yourself in deeper. Maybe see how he is when he next shows up for school. Assess the changes in him. Words aren't always the best way of healing a relationship, and it pays to be cautious, use restraint. Think it through and learn from what happened. I'm sorry you were left on your own and everything got so badly out of hand. We let you down. Thank you for telling me. I doubt very much the lad'll say anything to his parents, and if he doesn't I don't think you need to either. Sounds as though you gave him chastisement enough, without bringing down his father's wrath on his head as well. I think in all honesty I'd let it be, if I were you. But take it into your prayers, and so will I. Watch to see how things unfold."

Realizing he should have locked up the schoolroom – Brother Josephus usually does it – Damian goes back to get the key from its hook behind the door. Rounding the corner of the building, to his astonishment he finds the same child dawdling about outside, mooching along kicking at stones in the dust, evidently waiting for him.

He looks down on the grubby face, the only clean bits washed by the boy's own tears, his eyes still swollen from weeping.

"I'm sorry, Brother Damian," says the miscreant, to Damian's surprise. His anxiety plain to see as he plucks up courage, he begs, "Please don't tell my dad, or I'll catch it from him."

In the worried, upraised face, the monk sees the fears and affliction of childhood.

"Not if you'd rather I didn't," he says. "But look, it's your secret, not mine. And I'm glad you came back. I wanted to talk to you, because I think I frightened you, and I laid about you cruelly with that rod. I cannot have you go on as you did today, but I'm sorry too. I'm sorry I lost my temper. Shall we start again? Don't be scared to come back to school tomorrow; you won't still be in trouble. Try if you can to be a bit calmer than you were today."

Something is restored in both of them as they part company. Brother Damian, walking back to the claustral buildings of the monastery, reflects that though he came out of the world to this place to draw closer to God, the main thing he's found himself encountering is raw, uncompromised humanity – not least his own. He thinks maybe those two things aren't as distinct as he always assumed.

Chapter Sixteen

As the community disperses when the Office of None is concluded, Colin leaves the choir through the south transept, once more up the night stairs to the upper ranges of the cloister buildings, this time headed for the library in the west range – a peaceful and pleasant place to spend an afternoon, as the golden light of the September sun rays in through the tall, leaded windows with their uneven, greenish glass.

Father Theodore told him to report to Father Chad, the librarian, at some point after None. He thinks he might as well go directly there, before anyone catches sight of him and sends him off on some errand bound to take longer than they supposed.

Colin thinks about Father Chad as he climbs the stairs and walks along past the cells occupying the whole length of the south range. There's a problem. He cannot get out of his mind a casual remark made by his friend Bernard, who came with him from Escrick to try the life, but quickly concluded it was not for him. Too much routine and not very interesting. In the course of their first few days, Father Theodore put into Colin's hands a book of sermons they had been studying in the novitiate, saying: "Of your charity, would you take this up to Father Chad?" New and still permanently bewildered, Colin simply said, "Yes, Father. Should I go straight away?" When the answer was "Yes", he felt stupid about admitting he had no idea who (or where) Father Chad was.

Somehow he felt he ought to know. Holding the book, he stood outside the novitiate dithering, wondering where to take it. Then he spotted Bernard appearing at the top of the day stairs, coming back to the novitiate rooms from some errand.

"Thank God it's you!" Colin felt safe to confide his dilemma to his friend, who listened with amusement. "So," he asked Bernard, "where – and who – is Father Chad?"

Bernard grinned. "Father Chad? Hangs out in the library. We met him, remember? The world's most boring man."

Colin reflects that a lot has changed since he had that conversation. At the time he laughed. He wouldn't now. He realizes he's learned, from Father Theodore mainly but not only from him, different ideas about people and conversation. That if it isn't kind you don't say it – even if it's funny. That meanness has a way of worming itself right into your heart, dividing you from your brothers. That you don't say what you wouldn't want overheard. That you put yourself in the other man's shoes, and ask yourself, if it was me, how would that make me feel? All of this, and a lot more of the same kind of thing, he has heard from Father Theodore in good measure. He has come to see that what makes St Alcuin's such a special place to be is a mixture of respect and kindness; a practical compassion that goes gently in dealing with a man's ordinary human frailty, clothing him with dignity again and again, whatever his tendencies to fling off his robes of intelligent recollection and wallow in the mud of asininity.

And Father Theodore has been most particular to stress that it's not only what you say to your brothers, but what you say about them. It makes a difference to what lies between you, he assures them, even if they don't know what you've said. It muddies the honesty of love.

Now, walking along to the library, Colin remembers what Bernard said, and how funny he thought it at the time. In fact, from that moment on, every time he's seen Father Chad in chapel or in Chapter or in the refectory, even the back of him walking along the cloister, that's what comes to mind: *Oh, look. The world's most boring man.* It wouldn't be so bad, he thinks, if it were not so acutely observed. Because as far as he can see, it's unfortunately true. He supposes Father Chad has an interior life, a self coloured by fear and hope and sadness and imagination like everyone else: but no sign of it so far.

It lies between them, he thinks, as he opens the library door and enters its benevolent afternoon warmth and hazy golden light, looking about for the librarian. It's not something spoken or even (he hopes) guessed; but even so, it lies between them. Just like Father Theodore said such things do.

"Ah! Colin!" Genial and anxious to make him welcome, the world's most boring man appears through the big doorway connecting this shelved room full of books with the adjacent one. "Father Theodore told me you would be coming. He asked me to show you round. Obviously you've been in before – I mean, I've seen you here myself – but he wants me to make sure you know what we have and where to find it, and show you the best way to handle the books and how to put them away correctly so nothing gets damaged."

He shows the postulant the different sections: the collections of patristic commentaries, the lives of the saints, Bede's *Historia Ecclesiastica*, the herbals and books of medicine – Avicenna, Hildegarde of Bingen. There are several books by Augustine and Jerome, a number of books with homilies from long deceased abbots and the spiritual giants of Yorkshire in ancient times. There are some old records in a section for their domestic archives, in among them various oddments – prayers for the dying, a collection of recipes useful in Lent, a copy of the famous plan of St Gall. There are the books of legend with their spectacular maps and fantastical beasts, and a copy of the *Aberdeen Bestiary*.

"We have this psalter here – do you see? – kept with the books of legend. Sometimes it's hard to decide how to categorize things. The margin illustrations and illuminations of this one make up such an important bestiary of themselves, that we decided to keep it here rather than among the books of holy Scripture."

Father Chad turns the pages reverently, carefully, showing Colin the lions and bears and monkeys, the great leviathan, the camel and giraffe – and this enormous beast, called an elephant, with its flapping ears and almost unbelievable nose. "They do assure me," he says, marvelling, "that there really are such creatures in far-flung parts of the world. And unicorns like this. Amazing."

He explains the system in place for selecting books to take down to the carrels in the cloister for men's solitary reading in the afternoons, and which ones are usually chosen for reading in the refectory and at Collatio in the evening before Compline.

He stresses the importance of chaining the books, every single time, to the lectern desks: "They are so valuable, you see, Brother. Every one of these takes months of work, and some of them are worth a great deal of money. This library is a treasure house in so many ways – knowledge, inspiration, establishment in holy succession, and mundane material wealth. It is a great trust, and we must handle the books with proper respect. If a book gets torn or spoiled, assuredly we can copy it, but it won't be exactly the same – how could it be? Each one is crafted by the skill of the monk who made it. And that skill does vary, we have to admit. This one – see here..." He lifts down a book of hours and lays it on the table. "Compare with this one..." He fetches a bigger book, another horarium. He watches to see Colin's reaction, as the postulant turns the pages of first one then the other, with due care.

"Do you see the difference?"

Colin nods. "I do indeed. This one is a bit clumsy in places. The writing's uneven and hard to read. The colours are garish and the figures look absurd. But this – the little one – it's just exquisite! Everything marries together in such harmony, I haven't got the words to say it. So beautiful."

Father Chad listens, nodding in approval. "Do you know who made this lovely book, Colin? Of course you don't; how could you? It was started by our previous abbot, Peregrine du Fayel – Father Columba. Then those savage men attacked him and he lost the use of his hands. So he asked Father Theodore to finish it for him. You can hardly tell between the work of one man and the other. Consummate skill. And, you see what I mean? Irreplaceable. Father Columba is dead, and Father Theodore occupied with the care of the novitiate. Oh, yes, we could copy it, but do you see how we could never make one the same? I take this book down sometimes just to look through it and let it fill my soul – not only with beauty, but with the remembrance that everything passes, nothing is forever. Each ordinary day – it will never come again. And who ever knows what tomorrow will bring? When Abbot Columba laid aside the pages, half-finished, because of the call on his time made by Holy Week, little did he think that on Easter Monday his hands would be smashed beyond mending. So much sorrow in the masterful beauty of this little book, Colin, but also so much hope. Father Theodore finished it triumphantly, helped Father accomplish what he'd lost the ability to manage for himself. I always think there's a lesson in that. As there is in so many of the books here; they're like people, really – living beings. Only not quite so troublesome or contentious!"

He fastens the books back into their places in the racks with careful reverence, then shows Colin the section with poetry, and philosophy from ancient Greece and Rome. Colin remembers to mention the books Father Gilbert recommended, and Father Chad shows him where to find them. He asks what Colin's interests are, and enquires how things are going for him. Does he warm to what he finds so far? Is he enjoying it?

The postulant finds himself chatting away with enthusiasm, describing the diversity of occupations he's had the opportunity to try during the summer. Brother Walafrid took him along the farm track right up onto the moor, gathering herbs – showing him what to look out for, where the less common plants could be found. Then he learned how to dry them so no mould would form and their precious virtues be preserved.

Brother Stephen taught him how to mend a drystone wall, and he'd never done laundry in his life before he was sent to help Father Bernard. Brother Mark introduced him to the bees, and Brother Clement taught him how to grind the pigments to mix ink, how to combine them with powdered oak galls and ale and soot.

Then there were the familiar, homely tasks – dead-heading the roses with old Brother Fidelis, hauling muck from the stables for Brother Peter, helping Brother Conradus take down the finished pea haulm in the kitchen garden.

All the practical things, Father Chad observes. Is that where his heart lies, rather than in the mystical forays or the knotty intellectual problems? Colin thinks yes, that's probably so.

Father Chad, like the other men in full profession, is a good listener. Colin becomes aware of the attention and respect with which his ordinary tale of daily life is heard, as if it were of great interest, entirely captivating. It makes him feel happy.

"It's the little things, isn't it?" says the librarian thoughtfully. "Just the fragments and oddments. A moment's conversation in the warming room, incense smoke drifting up through an early morning sunbeam in chapel, the rise and fall of psalm chants at Vespers, the look on a man's face when his eyes are closed in prayer. A scrap of kindness, a snippet of friendliness, a gleam of insight here and there, a fleeting experience of grace. It all patches together somehow into a mosaic pattern of something dearly held, something that grows deep roots into a man's soul, so that his heart belongs here and nowhere else. It's in the stones, in the wood, in the air. But, dear me, it's not all charm and delight, is it? What are the things you've struggled with? There must be some – I know I've had my battles!"

Colin tells him how switching between work and prayer doesn't come easily to him – he likes to get stuck in to a job and see it through. The constant interruptions set him on edge, make him irritable. And he's got very tired at times, immersed in a completely new place, surrounded by men he doesn't know. It's worthwhile, yes; but sometimes he's felt very homesick. Father Chad listens to him, nodding in affirmation, kindness in his eyes. "Yes indeed – those things are hard. Adjustment. You find yourself longing for something familiar, something that comes easy to the hand. But you will – you know that, don't you? This place'll fit you like a worn-in pair of boots before you know it."

"What... what were the parts you found difficult, Father Chad, when you were new?"

"Me? Goodness, that's a long time ago. It feels now as if I've been here all my life. But my struggles have mostly been of my own making. I... well... I'm not a very *substantial* man, if you know what I mean. No scintillating wit whatsoever, and nothing much in the way of depth to my thoughts, either. I annoy people. I can be slow to catch on. And sometimes, I can give in to resentment, or take a dislike to someone. I'm a creature of habit; don't always find it easy to shake such things off; and I've been very, very mistaken in my judgment at times. I used to be the prior, as you know, but the bald truth is I was not really up to the responsibility. That's why Father John let me do this instead. You know, when I think about it, I'm not sure anything in my life has been worth calling a struggle or a battle, after all. It's only what it feels like inside."

Colin listens, intrigued, to this humble, quiet disclosing of personal truth. It has a feeling of authenticity about it. A man without affectation or pretension, not afraid even of his own inadequacy. The strength of spirit that requires, he thinks, must take a long time to develop. It couldn't come all at once. He wonders if this is what integrity looks like.

As they put away the books, and Colin thanks him and takes his leave, he reflects that he actually hasn't found Father Chad's company boring at all. Once you get to know him, he's just nice. Perhaps, as it turns out, Bernard was the boring one? But he shrugs that thought away as he walks back down the stairs leading to the cloister. He decides that categorizing people for their entertainment value is not an especially profitable exercise.

Chapter Seventeen

Brother Stephen knows this farm track like the back of his hand – possibly better. He could walk down it (or up it) in the darkness – and he often does, especially at lambing time.

The stretch his feet travel most is the path leading out from the east range of the cloister, past the infirmary, and up the hill to the main cluster of farm buildings. But the track wends beyond that, rising towards the moor and the extensive grazing grounds of the abbey sheep. Just now the cows are high in the top pasture. Wet summers have cursed the grain harvest most of this century, and plagues thrive in lingering damp, but at least the grass and meadow flowers grow lush in the watered hills. Now the grain is safely in, Stephen has stopped anxiously scanning the sky for clouds sailing across the valley with their cargo of rain, sensing the air for the telltale clamminess of arriving downpours. It's better, of course, if they can get it all threshed, winnowed, sieved, and bagged away while these dry winds hold good, but it's not the end of the world if the weather breaks now. In fact, some showers will bless the apple orchards, plump out the forming fruit of the late-ripening varieties.

The cows stand in a cluster, waiting for him. They don't have many, you could hardly call it a herd, just the eight milkers for their own use and whatever calves are running alongside their mothers. They concentrate on sheep; it's what the land's suited to, and the monastic life. The trading with the world is seasonal with sheep, daily with dairy farming. There's plenty of coming and going through the abbey gates as it is, but they have to make the choices that support a cloistered life, foster the separation from the hurly-burly into holy silence. For that, sheep represent a better choice than cows. But thirty-one monks, a gaggle of novices, and a drift of cottagers and villagers, between them get through plenty of cheese and butter. In fact, Stephen is mighty glad they had two heifer calves born this spring to grow on for enlarging their supply. These last weeks there have been mornings, and evenings too, when Brother Conradus has stood waiting at the door when he brings down the churns from the milking. Which is unusual. What's the matter? Why are they running short? The yields have been good.

"Come on then, ladies! On you go!" Brother Stephen opens the field gate. Ponderous, they come through on their cloven, planting feet, filing in their undeviating order along the track. He props the gate open, ready for their return after milking tomorrow morning, and turns to follow them. Cows slow you down, the peace of their passage through the world. He likes walking behind them to the milking shed, their tails occasionally swishing annoying flies away; likes their strong bodies and unhurried tread. The only skittish beast they'd had was the one Brother Tom picked out to give William – because she'd just come into milk for the first time, had many good years in her, was strong and healthy, and would milk through many a month before he had to think about the services of a bull. But she had a mind of her own, that cow. Well matched with William.

Now and then swinging a head, blowing, otherwise plodding calmly, the cows pick their way down the track. Brother Stephen sometimes thinks that if you cut him open and took out his guts, his heart, eviscerated the core of him, all you'd find inside him would be England – the green lanes, the lark and the curlew, the voices of sheep, the wild roses and sprays of blackberry, the sloes and the mountain ash. And low-growing plants, grass and chamomile, speedwell and shepherd's purse, yellow archangel and lady's smock. Over it all, the wide blue spaces of the sky. Celibate life in community suits Brother Stephen perfectly well. He likes silence and routine, and he can't cook. His faith in God is not something he can look at as a thing in itself – as his pulse and eyesight and digestion are part of him, so is his faith. As a beast breathes because it is born to, because it belongs to this living earth all wrapped and wreathed in air currents, so his soul turns to faith because it finds itself in God, his native air, his heart's true home. And his lady, his love, is this England, in her green dress, her careless trailing tresses, her subtle fragrance and sparkling necklaces of diamond dew.

We are, he thinks, born of earth; it is what we are. Vessels of clay, formed of dust made pliable by blood and tears. In the earth that is us falls the seed of God, his living word. And the roots of Christ's tree, the rood of our salvation, quest their feeling fingers down into the humble stuff of our mortality, and hold it strong.

He always starts this early. It takes a while to milk eight cows, however practised you are – then the milk has to be strained and the churns stacked in the barrows, the beasts let through to their yard with its byre, and the milking shed swilled down. Milk is only one end product of all that rich pasture and its stream-fed stone trough. The rest is the most spectacular splattering mess.

He takes his time. Rushing undoes itself, in Brother Stephen's opinion. The root of wellbeing is taking life gently; not shirking, just letting it find its own rhythm, its own way.

They know their places, find their own way in, stand waiting, one blowing out breath, one stamping a foot. He ties them and sets down feed in the mangers in front of them. Then he goes from cow to cow, washing them down, milking with practised, methodical hand, the stream of milk squirting hard against the side of the bound wooden pail. By and by, all are done. He unties the loose ropes from the row of forged iron rings fixed to the walls, and the big beasts back from their places, their chosen leader going first – an abbess cow, Stephen supposes, Mother Mary Matriarch. Our Lady of the horned and humble house-cow, pray for us. He fastens them into the foldyard, leaving them with hay in their nets in the byre. Water springs in all sorts of places up here in the hills, so the water trough looks after itself.

As he often does, lugging the milkpail through repeatedly, lifting it to tip into the churns, hefting them up onto the barrow, then filling the pail three times from the spring to swill the place clean, Brother Stephen thanks God for his body's strength. Nobody could call him a scholar, and his singing almost makes Father Gilbert cry. His lettering's not worth the waste of ink, and much preaching goes in one ear and out the other. But he does know the husbandry of beasts and the care of the land. He can recognize honey fungus and the first signs of foot rot. He can assess the quality of grain and select good animals for breeding. Weather wise, he knows when to put in the sickle and when to wait. The fields and flocks alike thrive under his care. And this is his worship, his service to God. This – his whole life – is what he lays on the altar stone, the bedrock of his being, his heart's love. Daily, faithfully, unquestioningly, he walks between foldyard and cloister, up and down this track that he loves, times beyond counting. Because he is sound in wind and limb, strong and able, knowledgeable, he has something he can contribute, a gift to bring. He feels secure in who he is, and aspires to nothing else. All Brother Stephen hopes and prays for is to be granted leave to spend his span of allotted days exactly like this; and at last, when life is done, to be laid to rest in the abbey's burial ground on the hillside, under the grass he and Brother Tom have mowed with their scythes, bounded by the wall he and Tom have patiently mended when it tumbled, under the tossing clouds, in the free air, in the rain and sunshine. There, he believes, he will sleep easy until Christ comes again.

His way down the hill, trundling the handbarrow with its churns, taking care to avoid any ruts that could throw it off balance or trap a wheel – though he and Tom are careful to fill in the big ones with stones – takes him past the infirmary buildings.

Glancing across as he goes by, he sees Brother Michael helping some old man to his feet – someone who has been sitting out in the sunshine these last golden days before the storms come and the year moves down into darkness. Father Gerald, it looks like from here. And Brother Stephen thinks how the curve of a life is not unlike the round of the year – you have your spring, your high summer, and you'd better make the best of it. If you have no harvest to bring in come Lammas, well, the frosty days and black nights ahead look almighty bleak. What sweetens the winter days is the warmth of a fire from wood you chopped earlier, a hot bowl of gruel or pottage from provender grown in the summer and set by. But then, he thinks, there's more to it than that. For how can you sow a field that isn't ploughed? Where will you build your fire with no house and no hearth? It's not only what you do yourself alone, it's what men before you built and laid down, how they lived – and it's what we all pull together to do. One man alone is very limited, however skilled and strong. Anyway, where would he get his skills from, or for that matter his tools, without those who walked before him and beside him? Life is short, very short. Not long enough even to provide for yourself without help.

Maybe, even, you could say a life is like a day – then by heaven, is that not a lottery? All of us have our morning and our noontide before the shadows lengthen and the night comes down – but some of us bask in sunshine while others have to hunch along through driving rain. What's with that? Without sun and rain, wind and weathers, no life can be. He's heard there are frozen lands where nothing grows, beyond even where the Vikings came from who settled in Yorkshire, ploughed it up, and sowed the seeds of their language everywhere. He's heard there are melting hot lands where rain never falls, where the earth is bare desert, and they travel along on camels like the Three Wise Men, their heads wrapped in cloths to protect from the merciless sun.

By the Mass, he thinks, as he stops his barrow on the flags near the kitchen door, *I'm glad I live in England. I'm grateful I've had the day and the life I have. It's the right one for me.*

Indoors, Brother Conradus is busy with his preparations for community supper. So Stephen carries the churns in for him to the kitchen dairy. It's at the back there, on the north-east side of the kitchen building. It has thick walls, small windows, and stone shelves, so everything stays cold, even on a warm day like this. It's all scrubbed clean in here, as neat and orderly as you could possibly wish. Conradus, thinks Stephen, is an excellent kitchener. He sets the churns of milk in the usual place on the Yorkstone flags of the floor, collects the scoured and rinsed empty ones from the morning left waiting for him by the door, loads them onto the barrow, and sets off on his last trip to the farm before Vespers.

Chapter Eighteen

Colin can hardly believe how much of a dogsbody a postulant has to be. Having been settled in no particular obedience, it sometimes feels as though thirty-one men share a consensus view that he obviously has nothing to do. Every request is courteously made – but firmly; nothing diffident or shy. "Colin, could you just take this laundry list across to the guesthouse… Colin, Brother Michael needs these tinctures I've made up; are you free to take them down to the infirmary?… Colin, of your charity, would you mind running over to the porter's lodge with these letters from Father John – he thinks someone will be coming by this afternoon who could take them for him… Colin, Brother Benedict has sent up some clothes from the infirmary needing alteration – will you be so kind as to trot upstairs to Father James and see what he can do?… Colin, Brother Boniface has hurt his foot. Nothing serious, but I've sent him to the infirmary for Brother Michael to take a look. Brother Conradus will be short in the kitchen, getting ready for supper. If you have time to give him a hand that will be a blessing… Ah, Colin, thank you so much for coming to help me – what a Godsend! Would you mind taking this list of things we need across to Brother Cormac? He'll need it before the end of the day, or I'd take it myself. God reward you – I really am most grateful."

"Oh, don't mention it! Shall I go right away?"

So here he goes bearing the kitchener's list of necessities across the abbey court towards the checker. As he approaches the door he hears the sound of conversation within; and hesitates. It sounds not entirely happy, has the abbot in it, and he thinks his intrusion with his errand might be unwelcome. It isn't that he means to be eavesdropping; he's only trying to assess what the proper course of action might be. After all, Brother Conradus did say the cellarer needs this before Vespers, and it won't be so very long before they're ringing the bell. What to do? So he listens carefully to the exchange between the abbot and the cellarer, trying to make up his mind whether to interrupt. Or not. And if not, what to do?

"I only ask you" – this is the abbot's voice, firm and level – "because I cannot help noticing the portions of poultry and fish served to the community are becoming smaller, and fewer; likewise the servings of cheese. Seeing this, I enquired in the infirmary, and I find their special allowance of beef tea has been halved. So I went back to Brother Conradus to ask why, and he tells me it is because less beef is made available for him to make it. Then I went across to the guesthouse – same story. Less cheese – but, oddly, no less butter. Half the capons they used to be provided with, half the chickens. No ducks and no mutton at all. Today when I asked for something to be set aside for men coming home late, I'm told we have plenty of bread, but not cheese, or cold chicken. Can you tell me what's going on? I mean, I can guess, but I want to hear you explain it yourself."

Calm. Kind. Colin can just imagine those steady brown eyes pinning the cellarer in place. He wonders if staying to listen is even more intrusive than dropping off his list and legging it out of there; but now he wants to hear the cellarer's answer. Abbot John may be able to guess what it's all about, but Colin can't. He presumes it must be an exercise of frugality. Maybe the money is short. For several moments, holding his breath and straining, agog, to hear, he finds himself listening to silence. And when a voice picks up the conversation, it's the abbot's again.

"Let me help you. I suspect this is no oversight in the ordering, nor shortage in our own supplies. Heavens, the place is fluttering with pigeons. Neither have you waxed unduly parsimonious. It's that you don't want to slaughter the animals or the birds. Am I right?"

Fascinated, Colin steals closer to the door, clutching his list and keeping well back by the wall where he cannot be seen by the men inside the small building. He glances briefly over his shoulder to be sure he's unobserved, but at this hour everybody's scrambling to finish off the day's work – the abbey court is deserted. He hears an indistinct murmur from whoever is not the abbot – Brother Cormac, presumably – then Father John again.

"Brother, you cannot do this. The obediences of the common life are not an opportunity for men to impose a personal philosophy on everyone else. The brothers need the strength and warmth that is in fowl and fish to stay fit and well. The frailer men in the infirmary need their beef tea to build them up. I understand how you feel about the taking of life, but you know, everything dies. While they live, we husband them kindly – they are fed, they have shelter and space. They do not bear the anxious search for safety and succour of wild birds and beasts. And the fish – well, glory! A fish will eat his neighbour's entire brood of offspring in one nonchalant gulp. They are not delicate in their sensibilities.

"Besides, even suppose we ate nothing but vegetables and grain – do you think there would be no cost of life? Did you imagine the men in the kitchen treat tenderly the caterpillars on the cabbage, the blackfly on the beans, even if you do? And have you deluded yourself the field mice would all escape the trample of the mowers and the blade of the scythe?"

From where Colin stands listening, the abbot seems to be talking entirely to himself. His reasonable, persistent arguments meet only silence. At this point, he would give a lot to be able to see Brother Cormac's face. The silence lengthens. Then, the abbot again: "And what's with cutting down on the cheese, for heaven's sake?"

Finally he discerns – low, unhappy – a reply from the cellarer.

"It's the calves. They're just babies. There's no point stinting our own milk, our own butter, is there? We have it anyway. But surely we don't need to buy in extra cheese, Father? Our cheese, our milk, our butter, our curds-and-whey – they come at the expense of a calf's death. Bad enough that we sell our own bull calves for veal; can we not leave it at that, and keep a little back for our beef tea – make what we have go round? Couldn't we be content with what our own cows give, and with things like apples and bread and beans?"

Colin's jaw drops. Their cellarer is a tough, uncompromising man. Nobody argues with him. His blue eyes, flinty, drill into you like gimlets. But here – and the voice is recognizably his – the pleading tremble of vulnerability is unmistakable.

"Cormac, I cannot let you go on with this." The abbot's voice is gentle. Colin feels the kindness of it like a pain. "Let me see your order books, Brother. Where is the list from the kitchen?"

With a guilty start, Colin looks down at that list clutched in his hand. The last thing he hears as he turns to go is the cellarer, humbly saying, "I'm sorry, John." There is something in the childlike sincerity of it that moves him more than he would ever have expected; it just catches at his heart. With absolute stealth, he backtracks to the middle of the abbey court, then re-approaches the checker, loudly humming his part to the Gloria.

He treads with determination up to the open door, walks in with the most guileless air he can muster, then stops, as if surprised, waving the list in his hand: "Oh! I'm so sorry, Father Abbot, Brother Cormac – I hope I'm not interrupting. Brother Conradus asked me to bring his list across from the kitchen."

He feels acutely the abbot's gaze on him as he says this; feels himself blushing to the roots of his hair. But what holds his attention most is the thing he wanted to see – the expression on the cellarer's face. Brother Cormac is not one to dissemble or put on appearances. Colin sees quite plainly the raw defencelessness still completely evident. Here is a man, he thinks, who would never pretend; and how rare is that?

Cormac leans forward, holding out his hand for the list. "Thank you," he says quietly, and Colin can see the uncovered soul in his face. He wants to comfort him, considers admitting he heard the conversation – but can all too well imagine how welcome that would be. As he puts the small sheet of vellum into the cellarer's hand, he remembers all of a sudden something Father Theodore said in their teaching circle no more than a few days ago: that there are times when silence is the best form of love. So he doesn't say anything more.

He remembers, just before it's too late, the small bow of respect due to his abbot. And then he leaves.

Walking slowly back towards the church, seeing as the Vespers bell will begin to ring any time now, Colin goes back into the conversation he has just heard. Like a man finding himself in a mysterious woodland, walking between the old trees, touching them, marvelling, hearing them sigh and stir, feeling their profound inner silence, so his mind explores the interaction, intrigued and wondering. He senses that he has come upon something intensely alive in the overheard encounter. His ordinary life before he came here included a lot of banter and repartee, and a great deal of activity. He had his work every day, and when that was done he would meet with friends, drink in the tavern – one song capping another, roaring laughter, jesting, clapping on the back. There were the lasses with their sidelong glances, finding it necessary to lean close over him, or looking back over their shoulders, tantalizing; and the lewd commentary replete with lively suggestions that followed them, among his associates. So much colour and vigour, so much to occupy body and mind in each brimming day; but nothing like this. He could not remember ever seeing a man's soul in his face as he had just seen Brother Cormac's. Nor ever hearing anything that touched him so deeply as the humble simplicity of the cellarer's apology to his abbot.

And then the abbot – watching Colin come in, quiet, observant. Pushing through his point with the cellarer, but never raising his voice, gentle.

Like someone putting out his hand for his finger-ends to touch and test the texture of an unknown substance, tasting it, gazing on it, Colin explores into what he has beheld. So small and fleeting, so unusual.

And he thinks back to his meeting with Father Chad; and the conversation with his novice master earlier in the day – the point at which he left. The bleak face, the glitter of sorrow in his eyes, the self-disciplined set of his mouth. *Scientem infirmitatem*,[20] Father Theodore had said to them, more than once, about Jesus – speaking to them of the immensity of those words, which he said could be rendered, perhaps, "immersing oneself in a course of study in what it means to be broken". He talked to them about it in the teaching circle, where he comes back again and again to the cost of the committed life; the treasure of faithfulness, and its agony too. The pain of loving, self-surrender.

An uneasy awareness begins to stir in Colin's viscera that if he goes ahead with his plan to make common cause with these men, he will be getting into something deeper than the wildest dreams his life has so far entertained. But if he doesn't, if he backs off it – too intense, too serious, way too holy – he will be losing something inestimable that he honestly believes he's unlikely to ever find again. Once more he comes back to the utterly humble simplicity of the cellarer's "I'm sorry, John". Its defenceless

---

20 Acquainted with grief (Isaiah 53:3, Vulgate)

candour makes him squirm, makes him want to run away. He cannot imagine being that open with anybody.

Then, behind him as he reaches the wide, shallow steps to the west door of the church, the footfall of a swift, decisive tread – and the abbot is at his side.

"Colin," he says, "did you hear my conversation with Brother Cormac?"

Mother of God! How does he know? All Colin's life so far has been a training in expediency. The canny thing to do in response to such a question is feign complete innocence, puzzlement: *I beg your pardon, Father – what conversation? Just now, you mean?*

It's as though he's suddenly in a different place. Not in this open court bounded by the mellow stone walls of the abbey buildings, but somewhere altogether less domesticated. Some kind of wilderness, in which the eyes of Christ, only partly obscured by the tangled locks of hair, the sweat and dust, the drying dripped blood, the crowning thorns, ask him: "Well?"

Because if nothing else, even if all the rest is alien and new to him, this much is clear: whatever these men are doing, the basis of it is truth. Anything less they will detect and discard. He can feel it. The abbot asks him, "Did you hear my conversation with Brother Cormac?" and Christ asks him, "Well?" And he sees the fork in the road, knowing that his "Yes" or his "No" is not about providing information but about giving his consent to take this way, to himself be *scientem infirmitatem*.

He stands quite still. He looks at the abbot. He hears in his own voice an oddly similar humble honesty as he just heard in Cormac's: "Yes."

He feels the same raw exposure as he waits to be scolded. He bends his head.

"Oh," says the abbot. "Then I think you will understand it was very personal and intended to be private. These things mean a lot to Brother Cormac. So, keep it to yourself, won't you?"

And that's all. The briefest of exchanges. But when he says, "Yes, Father, of course I will", the abbot sees he can trust this to be true. And when they walk into the church together for Vespers, the postulant knows that because of this day something has changed in him forever. Before, he was seeking and enquiring: now, he knows his feet are on the road.

Chapter Nineteen

"There! How's that? Good as new!" Brother Tom is pleased with the work he's done on William's scythe. "Sturdy. Blade's peened sharp as the Holy Spirit. I've made you a completely new snathe, fitted in the old grips – they were loose,. How you managed with those, God alone knows. I've wrapped them with twine, look; it's helpful for when your hands get sweaty."

"God bless you, Brother Thomas. I'm more grateful than I can say. That's such a big help." William examines it admiringly.

"Don't leave it there, then," says Madeleine, bringing the supper things through to the table; "at the foot of the stairs like that. Bound to be some lubberly dolt trips on his own feet and takes his leg off at the ankle."

"Oh!" Tom grins at her. "I notice you don't say '*her* own feet'."

"Aye – right," she says crisply. "There's a reason for that. Women look where they're going. Brothers, husband, if you want to wash your hands before we eat, I've left a bowl of warm water and a towel on the table in the scullery. You'll see it. William and me, we don't always bother, but I know it's what you do in the monastery. Personally, I'm content to wipe my hands clean on my apron, unless I'm tending to somebody sick."

William carries the scythe out to the shed, hanging it safely on the bracket he made for it high on the wall. His axes – both the big one for splitting wood and his little hand-axe – and his whetstone are out on the bench under the window. When he goes to investigate, he sees Tom has sharpened those for him as well. Grateful, he hangs them in their rightful places and tidies the stone away. It soothes his soul, having every tool well maintained, neatly stored and fit for purpose. "Everything in apple pie order," Tom had remarked earlier in the day when William showed him where to find what he needed. "Not that I'd expect anything less of you."

He finds them standing round the supper-table waiting for him when he comes back into the house. Tom asks him, "Will you say our grace, seeing it's your house, Brother?" Again in his heart that lurch of gratitude still to be included as a brother – which in truth he is. His vows, his ordination as priest, they are for life. His defection into the married state merely suspends them.

He bows his head, and his guests do the same. "*Oculi omnium in te sperant et tu das escam illorum in tempore oportuno aperis tu manum tuam et imples omne animal benedictione.*"[21] Over the table spread with food, quickly and unaffectedly he makes the sign of the cross. "*In nomine Patris et Filii, et Spiritus Sancti.*[22] Amen."

"Amen," respond Madeleine, Tom, and Cedd, and they sit down to eat.

"That's a nice blessing," comments Brother Cedd, proud of being able to understand the Latin. "It has all creation in it – 'every living thing'. 'Thou… fillest every living thing with blessing'. It's beautiful. Did you make it up?"

"I did not," says William, wary of allowing the novice to elevate him to some exceptionally exalted rank of piety. "It's in the Psalms, but I've forgotten which one. Butter with that?"

"'Thou fillest every living thing with blessing'?" Madeleine

---

21 Psalm 145 (RC Bible 144) verses 15–16: "The eyes of all wait upon thee, O Lord; thou givest them their meat in due season. Thou openest thine hand and fillest every living thing with blessing."
22 "In the name of the Father, the Son and the Holy Spirit."

pauses, the bread board in her hand, arrested in her gesture of offering bread to Brother Tom. "Is that what we just said?" She knows hardly any Latin beyond the *Pater Noster*, the other prayers of the rosary, and the Mass.

"We did." William takes the thing from her hand and sets it down in front of Brother Thomas. "Why?"

"Well, I agree with Brother Cedd the notion is beautiful – but I'm a little leery of you and every living thing. What does the rest of it mean?"

"The whole thing is '*The eyes of all wait upon thee, O Lord; thou givest them their meat in due season. Thou openest thine hand and fillest every living thing with blessing.*' What could possibly be wrong with that?"

Seeing the eyes of all three men are fixed on her expectantly, much like those of creation on God in the psalm, Madeleine feels bound to reply. "My husband," she says, her eyebrows raised in a prim expression of mock austerity, "gets up with first light to feed the beasts. He takes hay and grain to the cow, the horse, the goat, scraps to the chickens and the geese. Well and good – but he doesn't stop there; not William."

Now William realizes his secrets are about to be exposed. He turns his face aside, half embarrassed, his hand moves in a small gesture of remonstrance; but he doesn't mind too much.

"When he's fed and watered the creatures everyone would expect him to feed," she says, "he turns his attention to the others. He'll scavenge fish skin and meat fat as a treat for the crows. *Crows*, I say, you'll notice, not *crow* – for they know where to come. The pair we had has raised four young ones successfully this spring and – I do not deceive you – those birds brought every one as it fledged on a slow fly past to show our William. Brought every one while it still had the fluffy grey feathers of childhood to show it the place on the fence you have to perch if you want tidbits. Aye – you can believe it." This last she addresses to Brother Cedd's incredulous grin. He's not sure if she's telling the truth or only teasing.

"But that's not the end of it. Everyone else in the village throwing stones at the crows, our William saving them tidbits. But come the evening, he'll milk the cow and shut the chickens in safe, then what does he do? He takes a little bowl of yesterday's bread torn into scraps and soaked in milk – *for the fox*. Can you credit that? And if there's gristle or skin he can snick from a joint of meat he'll give that to the fox as well. Or the badger. Whichever comes first. In the dry days of summer he'll leave them a bowl of water beside the well. That's bad enough. Is it the end of it? No. I say to him, 'William, wherever there's water to drink put down, rats will make a home. If you leave scraps about like this' – and he puts out bread and fat for the songbirds, the hedgebirds too, in the winter and when they have young – 'we'll be getting mice too.' And does he stop? No. What does he say to me? Soft and low. 'I had a rat for a friend when I was a lad, Madeleine; when I slept in the storeroom, in the attic.' What was it again? '*Thou openest thine hand and fillest every living thing with blessing*?' Aye, tell me about it! You know what I think, Brother Thomas? He's spent too much time listening to your Brother Cormac. He has much to answer for in my estimation, that man. Like that crazy visionary across the sea in Italy – the one that preaches to the birds and calls the mouse his sister."

"Oh, yes." William reaches for the ale. "When we know better, don't we? *We* know she was really a shrew."

He sees her face, shocked into silence, the sudden flush. "Oh, I'm sorry, Madeleine, I'm sorry," he laughs. "I didn't mean – I'm sorry, my love. Was that too barbed a shaft?" He holds her gaze, rueful, questioning, playful. Is she all right?

"I'll warrant the fox knows to show her young where to come, the same as the crow," says Brother Tom. "I'm surprised you don't have every fox in Yorkshire joining you for dinner – bar the ones our Cormac's slipping filched morsels to, exactly as you suspect."

"What?" Brother Cedd looks at him in astonishment. "Brother Cormac *feeds the fox*? Does our abbot know?"

Tom and William both laugh. "Aye, he surely does. Our abbot," says Brother Tom, "knows when to turn a blind eye. There's not a lot you can do with Brother Cormac. The art of leadership starts with being realistic."

"Truth there," agrees William.

"It's a wonderful thing," Brother Tom observes, "a vision like a spark in the stubble, catching fire. First the moonstruck friar in Assisi, then our own crazy Cormac, now the paws and wings and twitching whiskers of all the vermin in England melting the heart of this hardbitten Augustinian."

"Yes, but – what about the chickens?" demands Cedd. "And the geese? And the pigeons?"

"What about them indeed, Brother – that's what I say!" Madeleine offers him some more cheese, and ladles pottage into his emptied bowl.

"You have to shut them in, that's all," says William: "and be watchful. The fox is shy and wary. She won't come too close when we're about, during the day. Besides, if all that's on offer to eat is the geese and the chickens, surely that's what she'll take. Throw her some scraps and it might save the life of a goose. Anyway, we wax so indignant about it, foxes taking the poultry – what did we plan to do but eat them ourselves? If we can eat them, why can't the fox?"

"Because the fox hasn't paid for their food and housing," his wife retorts. "And the fox will get excited in a hen coop and kill every bird for a laugh, then run away."

"Oh, aye," says William, "I know; but a fox will do that anyway. Is there any reason to think it encourages them when we feed them? I think: they have to eat something. If we put down scraps maybe they'll be happy with that. And…"

"Yes?" Brother Tom is listening to him, amused, intrigued. It seems plain this man and wife have gone this circuit countless times.

"Well… sometimes, I sit outside in the dusk, once the hens are shut in. I take the food for the fox, and sit on the ground nearby. If I'm quiet and still, if I do nothing to alarm her, she'll come and look at me – as near as I am to you. She stands in her russet, head lowered, gazing at me, curious, with her amber eyes. She… I think she's beautiful. Why should I want to hurt her, or chase her away? Same with the crow. I'll put out his food on the wall, but before he takes it he'll come and find me, perch to greet me. We have a little exchange – and only then does he go for his breakfast. Oh, I tell you, there's more civility and appreciation in animals than there is in much of the society of men. They…" He stops. He says so quietly they hardly hear it, "They are my friends. Besides, why shouldn't I feed them? I know well enough what it is to be regarded as vermin, driven off, shut out, left to do without while others sit down to eat. I don't care what animal they are. I just don't like the thought of them being hungry." He lifts his head again, defiant. "And if it's Cormac put me up to it, well God bless him. It's made my life gentler, made it sweeter, made me happier. What's wrong with that?"

"Nay, husband, I'm only teasing you," says Madeleine. "I wouldn't have you any different, and you know it. So long as you get out there in good time before dusk, and see to it those chickens are shut in. Slip up on that and you might find me a tad sour. Because if the vixen's been led to think what's in our yard is her supper, who can blame her for her mistake when what she finds there is a laying hen?" She reaches across to pour more ale in the novice's mug. "You look astounded, Brother Cedd. Are you not familiar with the ways of these men who call the beasts their brothers?"

The novice shakes his head. "I'm not," he says. "In truth, I never heard anything like it in all my life. I'll look differently at Brother Cormac from now on! At least… that is…" He hesitates. William and Brother Tom take note of his confusion, but pretend not to see. It sounds as though he will be coming home, after all.

Chapter Twenty

The cardinal Office; the hinge that begins to close the door on the day at the end of the afternoon and the beginning of evening. The sun sits low in the sky, flooding in through the great west window and the open door to fill the church with hazy amber light, the colour of silence and gentleness, the colour of kindness and peace, the colour of friendship. The community rises, the reader asks a blessing, the cantor sets the swell of the chant flowing in rhythm from one side of the choir to the other. And so the day quests towards its end.

Brother Cedd's stall is still empty. The abbot and novice master no longer question each other's glance. They are just waiting, hoping.

Vespers sung, the brethren filter through to the lavatorium to wash their hands, then into the frater for supper. Today, Brother Cedd should have been serving: no comment is made, beyond the novice master asking Brother Robert to take his turn.

The servers have set the dishes out for them, and Colin inspects their contents with more interest than usual. The bread and salad they always have, and small beer. Butter, a very modest allocation of soft white cheese, half an egg. Sometimes they would have a whole egg; it's only now Colin realizes he's looking at the results of the kitchener's efforts to make limited amounts stretch. Because they ate the eggs when they would have had chicken or fish, they're short on eggs now. Because the big cheeses in store have diminished substantially, they're on to what Brother Conradus can make in just a few days from their own herd's milk as it comes in. Colin can see what he's done to try and eke things out – given them a substantial portion of bread; made it with herbs and plenty of oil, so it tastes really good, and added to it a generous allowance of butter. There are big dishes of plums, baskets of apples, and bowls of blackberries on the tables. A really nice supper, in fact. The blackberries are shining, still wet. It took a long time to pick them, then, after he had, Conradus discovered in among them a considerable quantity of tiny, threadlike white caterpillars, hard to pick off. So he soaked them through the afternoon, then washed them through three waters; and he hopes that's been enough. He's set out bowls of whipped cream at intervals along the tables. His hope is that if any of the tiny larvae remain, they'll be mistaken for minute stray splashes of cream. Provided no one watches long enough to see them wriggle, they'll be none the wiser.

The tables range round the edge of the refectory, so the men opposite are some distance away; but this room is in the west range, and well lit at this hour of the day. As the reader – Brother Germanus, competent but rather quiet – goes through the biblical portion set for this evening, then on to the appointed section of commentary, Colin watches Brother Cormac across the room. Colin has his back to the wall set with tall windows to the abbey court. The rays of the low golden sun come slanting through; in some cases right into the eyes of the brothers opposite. This means he can watch Brother Cormac without the cellarer noticing. An interesting man. His black hair, streaked with grey, tousles in disorderly curls around his tonsure. His mouth is firm, decisive, and his jaw has a resolute set. The contours of his face are steadfast shading through to stubborn. Even across the room the blue of his eyes pierces like shards of ice. His black brows and long eyelashes somehow combine with that fierce blue to give the impression of spikes. You wouldn't argue with him, Colin thinks. You wouldn't even bother to try.

The man's hands, as he breaks his bread, are bony, long-fingered. But there is something fastidious in his touch, as there is also a quality in his face – something subdued... a... what? Colin searches for the feeling of it – nobility? Refinement? Dignity?... or... perhaps something more ordinary; that he feels chastened and unhappy. It could be that. As he watches, he sees the cellarer pick up his half egg and unobtrusively put it onto the plate of the man next to him – Brother Thaddeus. Colin wonders why he did that. Is it an objection to eating the egg – is this too a theft of life? Or is he feeling ashamed about the shortages he's created, and doing what he can to put things right? He strongly suspects Brother Cormac is not allowed to do what he just did. You're meant to eat what they give you. It's part of being grateful; it's about lowliness.

As Colin tears his bread, eats his own half egg, he reflects on the conversation he overheard standing outside the checker. Cormac's notion that they should respect the lives of beasts and birds is entirely new to him. Did not God put them on earth solely for man's use and pleasure, then? Could it be true that they have a point of view of their own? To slaughter the bull calves, to hook the fish from the stream, break the neck of the fattened capon – did that matter? He's never met anybody in all his life so far who advanced an even similar opinion.

He thinks back to what the abbot said – "These things mean a lot to Brother Cormac" – and something else begins to take shape in his mind.

He felt drawn to this community by what he saw in the brethren – their quiet courtesy, their erudition, the hospitality they offer, their tact and graciousness – so much that he admires, and aspires to learn and emulate. In the short time he's been here, he's found the novitiate a cheerful environment. His fellows are good company; reverent but capable of a prank, not slow with their jests nor very tolerant of sanctimonious piety. But still the solemns seem to earn the name: remote in their distant world of full profession they go about their day, and he's thought of them as "the community", "the brethren"; which, each one self-effacing, they seem to encourage.

But now he has the first glimmer of an insight into the reality – which is so obvious once he puts his mind to it – that they are only people. Human. Individual. Real. There isn't – and yet there is – such a thing as "the community". That is to say, its arising angel is entirely made up of the effort, the faith, the love, of these men. And if they are simply human, people after all, that means they are flawed and quirky. They must have their oddities like everyone does. Some will be easy for him to live with, others perhaps positively repellent. This was always true, of course it was, but right now as he watches Brother Cormac sitting in the sunbeam, surreptitiously slipping Brother Thaddeus his egg, it becomes startlingly clear. The community is not an *entity*. It's just human frailty in all its ordinariness stitched together with love. It's just thirty-one men finding the willingness and the courage to say "Yes", again and again and again.

✠ ✠ ✠

Surprisingly often, Abbot John has cause to reflect on how excellent an appointment is Father Francis as prior. *Why didn't I see it myself?* he often asks himself. *Why did it take William to notice that Francis would be the man?*

For in any Rule of any religious order you care to dip into, every detail of the character needed to make a good prior reads like a description of Father Francis. Patient and courteous and diligent? Why, yes he is. Kind and friendly, a peacemaker? Yes, that's Francis. Adaptable, sociable, humble, intelligent, gentle? All of that. Ready with his smile, tactful, pleasant, a good example as a Christian man? Indeed, he is. He can even speak French and is as much at ease with the aristocracy as with the common man. At first when you read the outline of what's expected in a prior, you begin to laugh and think, "Good luck with that – were you looking for an angel?" And then when you read through a second time, you can't help but notice: wait – but that's our Francis. That *is* what he's like.

Second only to the abbot, and often acting as his deputy, the prior has many duties. He doesn't check everyone's up for Nocturns nor take round the lantern in the night Office – at St Alcuin's, that's the sacristan's job. He does, after Compline, sprinkle them with holy water as they go past him to retire for the night; but he doesn't go so far as to herd them up like sheep and see to it that every man's in bed. That's not how they do it here. If some want to keep vigil after Compline has ended, that's up to them. And they, who have to be up again at 2.30 to pray, can usually be trusted to go to sleep.

But he does keep the keys to the cloister buildings, after locking them up last thing at night. It's about this that Father John comes looking for him on the way out of supper.

The abbot sounds slightly apologetic, looks faintly embarrassed. Another of Francis's impressive assortment of talents is that he's exceptionally good at reading people. Sensitive and diplomatic, he avoids putting them on the spot or dragging their vulnerability into the light. But he can't help noticing – in this instance – that the abbot is uncomfortable with how exposed this makes him feel; that having a novice go missing means so much to him.

"Francis – of your charity – would you delay locking up tonight? In fact, may I take the keys, because you'll obviously want to get some rest? I don't expect you to sit up waiting, but... I'm sure Brother Thomas will be home, it's not that. It's Brother Cedd.

I'd hate it if... I couldn't bear it if he – well – I keep thinking, if he changed his mind and came home, only to find we'd locked up and gone to bed. I'll ask Brother Martin to leave the postern door unbolted. But I won't leave us without a watchman; I'll stay up, I promise. And if he does come home, I'll secure everything then. So may I – just this once – may I take the keys?"

And Francis, understanding, obliging, goes directly to fetch them from their nail on the wall in the checker, brings them straight to his abbot, and gives them into his care.

"Am I... you don't think I'm being too indulgent?" John looks at him anxiously.

Francis smiles at him. "I believe it has good precedent in the New Testament," he says. "'How think ye? If a man have an hundred sheep, and one of them be gone astray, doth he not leave the ninety and nine, and goeth into the mountains, and seeketh that which is gone astray?'"[23]

John listens, reassured. "Yes," he says. "'*Venit enim Filius hominis salvare quod perierat.*'"[24] Then he stops, suddenly uncertain. "You don't think... I'm not meant to go and look for him?"

"Father," says Francis, calm and reasonable (as a prior should be), "better not be over-hasty. Give him some space. He's not yet made his solemn vows, and he isn't our prisoner. Just cut him some slack, stop worrying – see what the morning brings."

The abbot sees this makes sense, sees this is a sensible, moderate approach; in fact, exactly what you might hope for in a prior. Then he says one thing more, which to John is the best of all, because he really means it: "I'll be praying for you, John – and for him as well."

---

23 Matthew 18:12 KJV
24 Matthew 18:11 – "For the Son of Man is come to save that which was lost." (KJV)

Chapter Twenty-One

"So," says Brother Thomas, setting his emptied ale mug down with an air of decision. "Time to make a move. It's been grand to see you again, Madeleine, William – and my hearty thanks for your generous hospitality. Good bread, good ale, kind hearts, and a welcoming home. What more could a man ask? Still, if I'm not back for Compline our abbot will be asking why, so I'd best be on my way. Now, then: how about you, lad? What's happening? Are you coming with me, or have you something else in mind?"

He turns his gaze to look Brother Cedd in the eye; and waits for his answer. William says nothing, crumbling his bread in his fingers, looking down at his plate. Madeleine sits quietly, feeling a whole life hanging in the balance, knowing that even now he doesn't know what to choose. She becomes aware that neither Tom nor William is breathing. She realizes the reason she noticed is because she's stopped breathing too.

"Will it be all right to come home with you?" Cedd asks tentatively, and Madeleine smiles at the tension sighing out of them. Brother Tom's face lights up, happy and relieved. "All right? A bit better than 'all right' I should think! God be thanked! I thought for a minute there you were going to tell me you'd given up on us. Right then, lad; let's be stirring. The shadows are lengthening and we'll have to take it turn and turn about on our abbot's mare. She's a solid beast but I'm no slender sapling, and you're better than a shrimp yourself."

"Take my palfrey," says William quietly. "I'll come over and fetch her tomorrow. Nay, seriously" – he dismisses Brother Tom's protest before it gets a chance to start. "It'll be no trouble to me, and you've left it a bit late to be walking. I'll get her fettled up for you. It's the least I can do after all your help today."

Madeleine refuses their instinctive help to clear the table: "Nay, go on with you! You've worked hard all day, the pair of you. But thank you for thinking of it. Give Adam my love – I'll be along to see him before the winter."

They both look puzzled. "Who?" Then Tom's face clears. "Oh! Your brother! Adam was our abbot's name as a lad, Brother Cedd – before he took the cowl. Aye, for sure – and he greets you likewise, if I forgot to say."

The clopping of hooves out on the flags of the yard calls their attention. Tom ducks his head under the lintel of the house door – it's not so very low but he's tall as well as broad, and a tonsured man learns to think of his scalp. Outside in the golden light of evening, William stands waiting, the reins of their mounts one set in each hand.

"Safe journey," he says. "God be with you. I'll be up tomorrow." He flips over the iron latch to undo the gate, and pulls it right back so they can ride out together.

Nightmare, William's palfrey, is an even-tempered, cooperative beast, strong and willing. Grateful for the loan of her, the two monks make their way.

For the first mile or two, going one behind the other along the narrow lanes, they don't speak. Then, in a broad place where there's room to travel side by side, Brother Cedd (who's evidently been thinking) asks Tom: "Did you… did you ever have doubts about your vocation, Brother Thomas? Did you always know it was what you wanted, or were there times when you wavered?"

Tom considers this question carefully. It is, he knows, his responsibility as a fully professed brother to protect and nurture the vulnerable unfolding of a novice's vocation. He must also bear in mind that this lad, though he's taken his simple vows, has not yet made his solemn profession. He could still leave the community. This being the case, any information entrusted to him now could leave with him – and thereby be noised abroad. It pays to be cautious in confiding. Even so, he thinks it's likely true that it may help to have some insight into an older man's journey, to realize that we all stumble, we all waver. No one's vocation drops fully formed into his lap, rolling faultlessly through to a triumphant, unblemished conclusion. Obviously.

"You... you don't have to tell me if you don't want to." Cedd glances anxiously at Brother Tom, not sure why he isn't replying. Perhaps he didn't hear the question in the first place.

"I don't mind telling you," says Tom then. "I'm just thinking it through – what I'm free to disclose, what should be kept within the community. But... oh..." He shrugs. "Well – why not? All right, then. When I reached the same stage you're at now, I walked away too. With me, it was about a lass who came as a guest to the abbey. I fell in love. I went to find her."

Brother Cedd's eyebrows travel upwards and his jaw drops as he looks at Tom. A new thought occurs to him. These men, the black-robed community in full profession, with their grave and dignified demeanour as they filter with such sobriety into the choir or the chapter house – they are only people. Each one must have his struggles, his weaknesses, his personal history. He feels vaguely stupid that this revelation should have been so slow to arrive in his imaginative grasp.

"So... what happened?" he asks. "Didn't it work out?"

"Well, like you I'd made my simple vows to be Christ's man. I didn't want to break my promise. It's not that it didn't work out; she felt for me much as I did for her. Linnet was her name. Sweet

Linnet. She was lovely. Assuredly it was something I wanted; but I couldn't feel right about it, deep down. St Alcuin's was my home. So I came back."

"And your abbot then, he just accepted that? How long were you away for?"

"Oh, I was out quite a while. He had some searching questions, and then the community needed convincing I could still be trusted. The night I came back, he made sure I had a good sleep and a hearty breakfast, lent me his warm winter cloak – it was freezing, snow on the ground – and sent me out to ask admission. And then they made me wait. Three days, three nights. One bowl of soup. A mighty lot of snow and frost and ice-cold wind. Never been so starving cold in all my life. When they finally let me in to beg admittance, I folded up on the chapter house floor in a crumpled heap, and they carted me off to the infirmary. Back then Father John was not so very long professed himself. Brother Edward was our infirmarian in those days, and Brother John – as he was then – still finding his way with it. But he took good care of me."

The novice absorbs this story, impressed and alarmed. "Do you think... might that happen to me?" He looks extremely worried. Tom laughs.

"No. You've only been away a day. That's a minor blip of a very different magnitude from an extended love affair, don't you think? And besides, even if Father John did the exact same thing, the experience wouldn't have the same effect in September as it did in the middle of winter. You'd get through it."

"Yes," says the lad, still thinking about it. "Yes, of course." He lapses into silence. They ride along together, making good progress, as the sun sinks down towards the western rim of the sky.

"Did you... have you... since you came back, did you ever wish you hadn't? Has it been the thing you wanted, after all?"

Again, Tom weighs his answer. He thinks of Peregrine, and the journey they made together. He wonders how much it might be helpful to say, and what should be left unspoken. "I loved my abbot," he says eventually. "I was his esquire, as I am Father John's. But Abbot Columba – Father Peregrine, we used to call him – he needed help. He had a bad leg, needed a crutch to get about, and twisted hands. He was set upon, grievously hurt. His hands were broken, beyond mending. And you know how it is when someone needs your help; you get very close to them. You asked about doubt and vocation – well, *there* was a man who struggled, who wrestled with God. But though he doubted the worth of his own soul, and some of what he went through dragged him down to bitter darkness – almost broke him – he never wavered in his vision of Christ crucified. And he never wanted a different life. I loved him, and I learned from him. I guess you could say my vocation grew out of his faith like a weed grows out from a crack in a stone wall."

Then the novice asks what Tom hoped he wouldn't feel his way to finding. "So... wasn't it hard, after Abbot Columba died, to change your allegiance to Abbot John, and be his esquire instead? Didn't you find that upsetting?"

Honesty, Tom thinks, is usually the wisest course. "Short answer," he says: "yes, I did. But only because love and grief are very painful. Not because there's anything amiss with Father John. You see... Father Peregrine was my mentor, really. My guide. I was only a boy when I met him, and he made a deep impression on me. To a large extent, the man he was formed my faith, set my path. Whereas John – er, Father John – feels more like my friend. But you know, what's drawn us close – the thing that's been the seed of real, lasting love and brotherhood – has been struggle, vulnerability, human frailty, call it what you like. These are strong men, Brother Cedd. No spiritual wimp gets elected abbot. When they break, when they stumble – and they all do, make no mistake, they're only human – it grabs you by the very gut."

"Father Abbot – Father John – he's had his struggles too, hasn't he?" Cedd speaks timidly now, feeling himself to be encroaching on intimate and tender territory, even though the man in question isn't there to hear. "His mother," he says: "how she died. And his sister. Nobody told us in the novitiate exactly what happened. All we knew of it was bits he explained in Chapter. But we could see what it did to him."

"Oh, aye," says Tom. "That and plenty of other things to worry him and cause him to search his soul. He treads no easy path, that lad. It's why he needs us. Abbot he may be, but on another level of course he's only John. That's what we're here for in truth – to try to understand, to help a bit, offer what kindness we can. There are times when we, each one of us, need to know we have companions on the journey. It's not so much what the other man is to us, or what he does. More that we've taken the road together. Just that he's there, doing it with us. It's not that any other man can solve our problems or carry our cross. But having him simply be there, even if all he does is see past all our nonsense of silly attitudes and annoying habits to the soul of us. That's the thing about community: not to do any particular thing or live up to our expectations, but just to be there with us. Like you and me, taking this road together, seeing each other home. That's what it is."

"Father William…" Cedd pauses, turning these thoughts over in his mind. "He left. So that… is it a shameful thing? Did it feel like a betrayal you had to forgive?"

It surprises him when Brother Tom laughs. He looks at him, reads the affection and amusement as Tom contemplates the thought of William. "Ah, no, it wasn't him leaving that set me all at sixes and sevens," he says. "It was when he showed up in the first place that upset me. See, we have a history, me and William.

But we got through it and, it astonishes me to hear myself saying it, but we're the best of friends now. I look back and I think, how can that be? Just shows you shouldn't be too quick to judge a man. Take time to hear his side of the story. Walk a mile in his shoes. In the end, I guess, the faithful life isn't about any kind of moral superiority, but in noticing we're all only human. I was going to say we're all the same, but we're not that. Which is another wonder of community – the individuality, the human oddity. Endearing, irritating sometimes, just baffling on occasion. But when you see a man's soul stripped bare, see him reduced by circumstances, exposed and defenceless, how can you help but love him?"

"When we are in our teaching circle in the novitiate," Cedd confides, "I sometimes look at Father Theodore and wonder who he really is, if you see what I mean. He's so calm and so wise. He's gentle, but none of us gets away with anything. He can be very direct. And I wonder what made him, what path he travelled. I suppose he had his struggles too."

"Father Theodore? Indeed he did. Nobody had a harder time in the novitiate, that I know of. Our novice master didn't care for him one little bit. He – Theodore – he had the same problem so many of us have. Thought he was no good, useless. Ended up sobbing uncontrollably on our abbot's floor, in complete despair."

Cedd gapes at him. "Father *Theodore*?"

"Aye," says Tom: "him. So who knows? If you stick at it, mayhap you'll be our next novice master one of these days. Anyway, come on, lad. Time we picked up a bit of speed. The sun's right down on the horizon. Nearly home. Let's see what these beasts can do."

Chapter Twenty-Two

After Vespers, there's this space before it's time to gather for Collatio and then into Compline. Not long. The professed brothers will gather in the calefactory, or maybe go for a stroll in these warmer months of the year. It's a beautiful evening.

There's a fireplace in the novitiate. The teaching circle of benches and low stools is broken up as the young men take them to gather round the hearth.

Colin usually looks forward to this convivial hour among his new friends before it's time to go down to the cloister. But not tonight. Vivid impressions and pictures from the day move around inside him like rustling forest creatures, glimpsed and lost. This day… he feels like a man who put his hand unthinking on a mound in the grass he hadn't looked at properly, only to feel it furry and breathing, warm to his touch. With a heartbeat. This day has overflowed with life. Music. Faces. Voices. Beauty. Mystery. Kindness. The curious individuality of men, in their human struggle to bring forth a faithful life.

So instead of heading inside to find the others, after Vespers he wanders slowly along the cloister to find some solitary peace. He walks the length of the west range, past the refectory, the little parlour, and the abbot's house which wraps round to form part of the south range under the dorter. Where the south range meets the east range an archway opens out towards the river. As he strolls that way, alongside the kitchen garden and the orchard, Colin wonders why on earth the past monks who built the abbey sited the refectory in the west range instead of the south. It ought to be handy for the kitchen buildings that jut out from the east range. They shouldn't have to trundle things back and forth as they do; it's a daily inconvenience. That's seriously bad planning, he thinks. He wonders if, in the old days, in the abbey's beginning, that storage room in the east range just off the kitchen might have been the original refectory. The big room next to the buttery. Probably – it has a nice arched ceiling and very lofty windows. Perhaps they moved it when numbers grew. If you're going to have lots of men, why not make things as awkward as you possibly can? Good for them. So what's now the frater used to be... what? Not the library. Nobody in their right mind would leave books so accessible to people drifting through, just off the abbey court like that. Anyway, the library in its present location, upstairs, has the air of establishment; the shelves are old, the nails in the wall well rusted. He tucks it away as something to ask the novice master in the morning.

He decides not to go to the left, beside the riverbank up towards the spinney and the burial ground, the farm and the moorland above, because that's a favourite walk for many of the brothers, and this evening he wants to be on his own. So he turns to walk along the path by the huge storage rooms, built like caves into the side of the hill as the land slopes down the valley flank to the river. Part buried, each having only one big window facing the river, they stay cool – and in some cases usefully damp – even on this south-facing side of the square. The sun serves to keep most of them tolerably dried out. It works well.

The path snakes on into the birch grove at the back of the abbot's house. These trees are so graceful, incarnating inspiration and peace in their whispering, leafy, arising height. He notices, somewhat to his annoyance because he craves solitude, a brother sitting on the low bench there under the tree. Then he stops short as he realizes it's the abbot, and now it suddenly occurs to him that here, right behind his house, is probably where Father John seeks refuge and takes much needed time to be alone. In fact it's quite possible this could be a place hardly anyone goes, in tacit agreement that their abbot should be allowed a bit of privacy. He would have turned right round and walked away if it hadn't been that the abbot has seen him, lifted his hand in a friendly wave. So now he doesn't know what to do. Walk past? Go back? Speak to him? They're not in silence yet.

Accepting that it would on balance look very rude to turn on his heel and head in the opposite direction, Colin decides the best thing to do is greet him and be honest about not having known this to be private space.

The simple humility of the cellarer's apology is still sending ripples from the centre of his being to its periphery and back, but obviously "I'm sorry, John" would be most impertinent coming from a postulant. So, as he comes near, he settles for a humble "I'm sorry, Father" by way of greeting.

"What? Why?" says his abbot.

"I hadn't the wit to see this patch of land at the back of your house is for your private use. I didn't mean to blunder in and disturb you."

His abbot smiles. The serious face, verging on stern much of the time, is warmed and illuminated by kindness that seems to emerge and envelop Colin like a hug.

"Don't you worry," he says. "Think nothing of it." From which Colin correctly infers that he was right, and he shouldn't have strayed along into this grove. "There's no private property here. Come and sit down."

Colin hasn't been long in this monastic community, but it has been early made clear to him that when the abbot suggests, or invites, you don't say no. It's a command. He's just putting it courteously.

Father John shifts along from the middle of the bench to make enough room for him to be comfortable. "You look pensive," he says. "Everything all right?"

"Oh, yes, Father – it's just been one of those days when I've seen so much and learned and felt so much, taken such a lot on board, that I thought my head would burst. I think, in truth, this has been a turning point for me – making up my mind that this is the right place for me. This is where I want to be."

He glances shyly at the abbot for his reaction, and is encouraged to see the evident gladness his words have brought.

"That's good to hear," Abbot John says quietly. "I won't say more than that, because you must have space to change your mind if you think differently later. But – well, it brings me joy."

"What..." Colin plucks up courage to ask: "What were you thinking about?"

"Me?" The abbot gazes out through the trees with their beautiful dappling light to where the low sun reflects golden on the river. "Well, oddly enough, I was thinking about my own first weeks and months in our community. When I was a novice and, before that, a postulant. The things I liked, and what I found hard to adjust to. We – I came here before the time of Father Peregrine – we had Father Gregory of the Resurrection for our abbot then; a sensible, practical man. Very sane. I was thinking back to a conversation I had with him. Something I didn't get on with at all in the early days was all the ritual and ceremony. I mean, I was used to the Mass of course, like everybody, so I expected to bow and genuflect and make the sign of the cross and all of that. But I didn't get on so well with there being a correct way of doing every blessed thing – a form of words, a prescribed action, when you could, when you couldn't, what you had to... I felt as though I'd been caught and caged, a wild animal used to ranging the moor and the forest, prodded and schooled into performing a whole lot of tricks. And I said as much to Father Gregory.

"He listened patiently, God bless him. I think I might have been very rude in the way I expressed myself, but he didn't chide me. He just listened, and commented in that mild, vague way he had, that if I liked I could try to see all these things we did as reminders. Useful, like notes to myself that I didn't have to bother carting around and sorting through, because the life did the reminding for me. He said there's only one trick really, and that's getting the knack of seeing more deeply into the meaning of all the little things we do. Like learning to say 'our book' and 'our spoon', instead of 'mine' – it's to remind us we are vowed to own nothing. That we have chosen simplicity, holy poverty. And then we can look deeper again, to remember that we belong to Christ; we are his property and at his disposal. We do not own because we are owned. And he said there is more peace in that than hardship; it is such a blessing and a relief to put everything down – all the cares of the world, all the troubles – and find rest in Christ, the one to whom we belong.

"He said the bowing, the kneeling, is for remembering humility – and is not that the most beautiful thing in the world? And the forms of address – Father, Brother – they are to comfort us with the reminder that this is our family. We have made a commitment to one another. This is no mere acquaintanceship or passing encounter. We have made one another our kin. Oh, and so much else he said, Colin. But for fear of boring you and because I haven't forgotten you came down here seeking solitude, only to find me drivelling on about how things were In My Day, I think I'd better stop. I guess the main thing he meant was that I, by nature impatient and all too inclined to be dismissive, would do well to learn to look more deeply before I tossed aside treasure I hadn't understood. And that's a lesson I've gone on learning – oh my, is it not!"

They sit in silence then. Colin wonders what he's supposed to do now. Should he go? Must he wait to be dismissed? A small, whirling cloud of midges catches his eye, the dance of their tiny wings reflecting the sun in sparks of gold over the river shallows just beyond the trees.

Time passes, and the abbot does not speak. As they sit there in quietness, Colin thinks how unusual this is. People generally feel obliged to make conversation. Silence is normally something awkward, prompting jests and adages and nervous laughter. But his abbot just lets it be. In his company, the peace he had hoped to find in solitude begins to seep into Colin's soul. As the sun dips low – crimson, vermilion, lilac, blue-green – the light fades from the day and the shadows intensify, he becomes aware in the cooling air of the human body warmth of the man sitting so close beside him. Sitting there together, the postulant has a sense of getting to know him – becoming acquainted with the colour... flavour... quality... of his soul. In the quiet dusk it emanates from him as distinctly as the aroma of an animal. Personality. Human being. And then the sun slips below the horizon and here beneath the trees chill shadows gather. In peaceful resonance, clear, measured, sonorous, the bell begins to ring.

"Oh! Rats!" The abbot sits forward, then jumps to his feet. "I must just run across to the gatehouse and have a word with Brother Martin; tell him not to – er – see you later, Colin – good to have a moment to talk."

And before the postulant has the chance to stand up as he should when his superior rises, and bow and do everything properly the way he's been taught, with a flurry of robes and a stride that almost breaks into a run, the abbot is gone.

Chapter Twenty-Three

The sun slides low in the west, bathing in a sky of vermilion, turquoise, gold, and dusky lavender. Time inches down into shadow. Mystery lengthens beneath the trees and gathers in the corners of the yard at Caldbeck, between the barn and the goatshed, between the stable and the house, in the well with its coolness and silence, under the henhouse. Rooks call from tall branches, and every now and then the voice of a sheep carries across the valley, and is answered by another. Crickets sing, still, in the grass.

Having seen his guests on their way, William turns his attention to the evening chores, alone with his thoughts. He prefers it that way. If Madeleine helps him, he has to choose between getting the jobs done methodically, nothing overlooked, and remembering the courtesies that maintain domestic harmony. He loves his wife and is glad of the life he has chosen; Caldbeck feels like home now, like a protective fleece drawn close about him against the uncompromising, difficult realities of life – the people and places he must avoid, the background pulse of threat and hostility. Much of his own making, he acknowledges freely, but it chafes his soul raw at times.

The fox will be about before sundown, stealthily opportunistic – much like himself, thinks William. So the hens must be shut in first. He checks. Yes, they are roosting; numbers up to six again. They lost all but two to the fox at the end of the winter, but neighbours have been willing to trade pullets for butter and cheese – not fruit, they had plenty of their own. So now there are six, brown and white and speckled, eyes drowsing, combs flopping, heads tucked down into fluffed feathers, in the gloom of the roost. He closes and bolts the door, and the little pop-hole door for their own use.

He fetches from the scullery a can for goat's milk, a larger pail for cow's milk, and a washing pail and cloth. In the quiet of evening the turning of the handle, to draw up water from the well, rattles loud.

Fetching in the goat is a patient, tedious business. She thinks it's a game. Happily she's also greedy, and the lure of oats shaken in her basin proves irresistible. Every evening he does this – taking the bowl into the furthest corner of her well-strawed stall, pretending to be entirely absorbed with some detail of the hay net until curiosity overcomes her and she approaches closer... closer... to look, while he ignores her. Finally, as her slotted eyes are peering past him and her pink nose is right against his hip, quick as lightning he grabs her collar. Some evenings she is even faster and makes a break for freedom so that he has to start all over again; but tonight he is successful, and glad of that because he's tired.

One hand holding her collar, the other holding the bowl of oats out of reach, he leads her to the milking stand. She hops up, twisting round to see the oats; he fastens her securely, gives the clean, pink udder a cursory wipe with the cloth, and lets her have the supper she's waiting for.

She knows him well, and lets her milk down easy for him; it flows plentifully into the can, not far from the top once she's all stripped out. He leaves her tied up while he takes the can into the scullery; he's lost too many pots of milk letting the goat get down first.

Then he comes back and unties her, settles her into her stall, sees to it she has hay and water for the night, scratches her bony forehead in the place she likes, pats her neck, crooning to her the endearments that make a goat happy.

He shuts her in until the morning and goes in search of their cow. This is a beast with a sense of humour. He knows what will happen; it's a new trick she has.

She'll be waiting for him out on the common, and come towards him as he goes to meet her, calling. He'll begin to drive her homeward, leisurely along the track, watching the stolid planting of her cloven hooves spreading under her impressive weight, marvelling at the dainty grace of her ankles, enjoying the sway of her belly and the rhythm of her walk. And then, at a particular point along the path, she'll dance sideways, cantering wildly down the bank, udder swinging, head tossing. What is she like, this cow? He has to follow her down, call her again, until at last she's had enough of it, consenting as the shadows lengthen and the air breathes a chill, to come into the cowshed and her milking stall.

He never ties her. She munches on the grain and the gathered comfrey he has for her, while he sits, head pressed in the hollow between her round belly and her sloping flank, squatting on the low milking stool, giving himself to the firmer, pulling rhythm of milking a cow. She, too, has established a bond with him, and her milk flows comfortably at his touch. He sets about it, giving her no time to get bored. If it takes too long, she'll just plant one foot firmly in the pail, swing about and walk off. He really doesn't know why he never bothers to tie her, racing against her boredom to finish up; that's just how it is.

And then, the milking done, the two pails left in the scullery where Madeleine will strain the milk through a cheesecloth into clean bowls for the cream to rise, he goes to find a heel of bread, tears it into a bowl and adds a slop of milk, then goes back outside.

He closes the house door behind him, and sets out in the dusk to walk the bounds of their homestead, check all is well, and set his little supper out for the vixen.

As he saunters quietly through the gathering dusk, he thinks of the day gone, wonders if Brother Tom and Brother Cedd are nearly home, and what reception the novice will find with his abbot. *Go gently with him, John,* he thinks; *God knows, we're all confused, all lose our way.*

He revisits his own conversation with Brother Cedd in the apple loft, and feels ashamed he couldn't do it any better; that he has so little warmth, such a horror of personal involvement. He didn't like the mention of his helpless tears, didn't want to have to recall those times of such strain and turmoil. He wonders what life will hold for Brother Cedd, knotted up inside and hungry for affirmation – afflictions of youth.

He thinks of his own life, so many years using the monastic system to obtain some measure of sanctuary and peace after a rocky beginning to his years on earth. *Why did God do that?* he wonders. *What possible good purpose could there be in it, for him or for me, to put me through a childhood of such unremitting wretched misery? What was it for?* Then he wonders if perhaps it had no design to it at all, it just fell out that way, for him to make the best of it he could, crawl out of it into the lap of grace.

He pauses, looking up the wooded hillside at the now black silhouette of the treetops against the last light in the west. The evening star is shining, very bright.

He thinks about the contrasts in his life, and admits the truth of it, that he began this marriage too old; he will always be a monk who got married, neither one thing nor another. Not that he ever was; for he never felt any kind of call before he fell in love. Perhaps he was born to belong nowhere, to be neither one kind of man nor another, just a feral soul set loose on earth as isolated and separate as that star.

And now he wonders what happens when you die. He sifts through the teaching of the church that has saints organized into serried ranks wearing crowns and white robes, shouting hosanna in a glittering city where night never falls and the praise never ends and nobody falls asleep any more. Where the relief of tears and the comfort of making love, the smell of night-scented stocks and the peace of watching the stars through the window as you fall asleep, is all over. Only the loud hosannas and the crystal city, or the exquisite inescapable agony of endless fire.

What a choice, eh? What a God. He wonders which fate will be his, and how a man could possibly tell. He thinks of the Gospel stories, of the separation of sheep from goat, so indistinguishable that even they are surprised to discover which breed they've been all along.

He thinks of the criteria. *I was naked and you clothed me, sick and in prison and you visited me, hungry and you fed me*; and he concludes that his future destiny is looking bleak.

He wonders how much of it you have to do. If there were ten sick men and you visited five, would you go to heaven for the five you visited or to hell for the five you ignored? Did it matter which way round it was – which you did most recently?

He looks up at the evening star, feels the cool of the night wind against his face and neck, then he closes his eyes. "Jesus... oh Jesus..." he whispers; "save me from myself. Save me from the weariness and confusion that dogs me always. Save me from cynicism, save me from despair. Set out of reach my tendency for cruelty. Set far from me the coldness that seizes my heart. Help me to keep my feet in the way of faith. Cling to me, Lord Jesus, for I have neither the strength nor the intelligence to cling to thee. Oh Christ, I beg thee, do not let me go. Do not let me fall into darkness. Do not let me be lost entirely. Take not thy Holy Spirit from me."

He thinks he might cry if he stays here any longer, probing

his chronic dread and distrust of life, so he finishes his prowling of the perimeter of his home, ending up by the walled vegetable garden, coming along the path dividing the orderly beds out through the arch into the flagged front yard.

Now night is deepening, and one by one across the darkening sky, the stars are coming out. He thinks Brother Tom and Brother Cedd will be safe home by now. It must be not far off time for Compline. In these last weeks before Michaelmas, they'll still be on summer timing. Compline will begin in darkness at eight o'clock, until they change to the winter ordering of things, bringing the day's last Office forward to a quarter past six.

He thinks of their life, shaped as regularly as breathing by the rhythm of prayer, the calm chanting of canticles and psalms, work quietly and mindfully undertaken, the study of Scripture and teachings of Holy Church, the mysteries of the sacred Eucharist and the prayers of the rosary. He wonders if they are, sort of, starting heaven in advance.

And then he begins to wonder again what happens when you die; if maybe after all it is only an ending, cessation. To his surprise, this provokes no fear in him; he doesn't care. He feels at peace with leaving such matters in the hands of God. One thing he fears now – well, apart from being some day tracked down by the ecclesiastical courts, tortured, and hanged for his sin in attempting suicide when utter despair overwhelmed him. Apart from that; one thing he fears only – that he will lose the way, let go of Christ's hand, become a hard empty shell with the softness beaten and eaten out of him by the hard-beaked predators of night. "Jesus... ah, Jesus..." he says again, softly; "for thy love's sake, do not let me go."

He hears the click of the latch and his house door opens, candlelight spilling out in a quiet glow against enveloping dark. He moves towards his wife, standing silhouetted in the entryway, wondering where he is.

Whether or not there is holy purpose in his love, he can't be sure; but he knows it has brought him alive; given him – as far as anything can give this to his scarred and twisted soul – a sense of belonging, a sense of home.

Chapter
Twenty-Four

Oh, no. The prior absolutely knows the meaning of that look in Brother Thaddeus's eye, as he threads his way towards Francis through the knots of men relaxing in the calefactory, his mug of ale in his hand. It is the kind of look the word "beeline" was made for.

It is so predictable he could have said it for him: "Fancy a game of chess?"

Francis wishes with all his heart the man wouldn't always pick on him. With childlike optimism Thaddeus is convinced he will win one day. He thinks he's improving. He challenges Francis several times every week. He loses every time and immediately wants to try again. But to his immense disappointment the prior will only give him one go.

"Look – Thaddeus" – in occasional moments of frustration Francis tries to explain – "it's not – you can't just make it up as you go along. You've got to be strategic. That's the whole point of chess."

Thaddeus has heard this is so, but isn't quite sure what that might mean in practice. If he's honest, it's the excitement of moving nobility around the battlefield – the oddly unwieldy knights in armour, the daring and rapacious queens – that's what fires his imagination and makes it so exciting.

He always wants the red army, because red is his favourite

colour. He'd love to make some red pots like some of the ones they make in Scarborough, but so far Abbot John has said "no". When Thaddeus asked him again last week if he could have some red glaze, he stopped and fixed him firmly in the eye, saying: "Show me *one pot* you've made that's good enough to sell in the marketplace, and I'll reconsider. We're not making red pots for use in the monastery because all ours are to eat off. And before you start badgering me – I did ask Brother Cormac and he says the red glaze is poisonous."

Thaddeus had taken those words silently into chapel with him, feeling hurt as well as disappointed. He thought his pots were all right. What was the matter with them?

Taking the red chess pieces in his hand offers a tiny consolation. For a few brief minutes, a whole realm of scarlet is at his command. And, for some mysterious reason he can never really fathom, he knows it *will* be brief. He has never won a single game against Francis yet. Maybe tonight.

Thaddeus moves out a pawn – any pawn, he has nothing in mind. The one in front of his bishop as it happens. Across the board, Francis moves out the pawn in front of his queen. Thaddeus counters with the same thing, and the two pawns stand head to head. Francis moves the pawn in front of his king out one cautious square.

Because Francis often brings a knight out early, Thaddeus thinks he'll do that next. So he does – realizing after he's done it that Francis's first pawn is now in danger. He's all poised to take it, then looks to see the implications of Francis now moving out a knight too. Oh. If he has the pawn, Francis'll take the knight. Bother. For no particular reason, he brings out his second knight, randomly. Francis brings his bishop streaking down the board. It dawns on Thaddeus that if he leaves the knight where it is the bishop can take it, but he can't move the knight without exposing the king. He chews his lip. Realizing he's going to have to sacrifice the knight, he moves his queen forward to bag the bishop – then wishes he'd moved his bishop in case he's put the queen in danger – he has no idea if he might have done; you never know with Francis.

To his surprise, Francis doesn't take the knight; he moves forward another pawn. Why? Now Thaddeus doesn't know what to do. He can't still get his knight out of the way without leaving the queen wide open. While he thinks how to respond, Francis waits patiently, takes a swig of his ale to pass the time.

Thaddeus moves a pawn out on the edge of the board, expecting Francis to give up on the knight and take his now surrounded bishop to safety. Francis moves a knight forward; Thaddeus sees this means he now has no option but to shift his queen or lose her. He carries her back to safety, and Francis's knight slaughters his. So he bags Francis's knight with his pawn – he has to, or the black knight can take his queen. But this leaves the queen vulnerable to the black bishop. He takes her back a square – only to have the black bishop take his rook. He hadn't even noticed it was in danger.

With a sudden clutch of fear he spots the relationship between that knight and his king – oh, but they're both his so it doesn't matter. So he slaughters the evil bishop with his queen. A black pawn takes his in the middle of the board. He sends his queen in retaliation, wondering if that will work out well or create some unsuspected exposure. Francis moves his king sideways. Why? Thaddeus begins to feel nervous. It's usually at this point that things start to go badly wrong. Tentatively, he moves one pawn one square forward. Francis brings his queen across the board, and now she is staring boldly down the diagonal, looking the red queen right in the eye. She sidesteps. Francis brings his queen right down to threaten the red king. Thaddeus has to move him immediately or lose; this will be the end of his bishop, but he does it. Francis isn't that silly, though. If he takes that bishop,

Thaddeus will have his queen. He moves out a pawn. Thaddeus, worrying about his bishop, barely spares that a glance. If he moves the bishop, she'll take his rook. He does, even so, because a bishop is more useful than a castle – ooh – he thinks Father John might be able to find a homily in that.

Francis leaves his rook in peace, taking the queen back up the board. Thaddeus is worried he may be overlooking something. He takes refuge in defence, moving his king back to safety. Francis brings out another knight. Does this matter? He has no idea. He moves his king. The black knight comes closer. He suddenly realizes that with one audacious move right across the board he can take the pawn protecting the black king with his queen. Oh no – wait – if he does that, the black king will simply take his queen. No, that would be silly. He frowns at the board. He moves his queen back into the corner, not sure what else to do.

He glances across the room at Brother Giles telling Cormac a joke, then looks back. "What did you just do?"

"I moved my queen – there," says Francis, patiently.

Thaddeus backs up his king. Francis brings the black queen down to threaten the king. So he can take her – but no, wait – if he does that, his king will be exposed to the black knight. Francis must have noticed and done it on purpose. He moves his king, Francis moves his queen one square. Whatever's he planning? He moves his king again. Francis brings the black queen down to the corner. Thaddeus suddenly realizes that moving the king now will leave his queen exposed. He has to do it. But Francis doesn't want to lose his queen either. Relieved, but not sure what to do next, Thaddeus moves his queen up next to the king. And the black queen takes the pawn standing in between her and the bishop. The other side of that bishop stands the king and then the queen. Panicking, Thaddeus accepts he'll just have to lose the bishop, and shifts his king.

"Not there," says Francis quietly before he puts down the

piece. Oh. Thaddeus realizes if he does that the knight can take his king. Francis is gentle in his application of the rules in these futile tussles. So long as Thaddeus hasn't actually put his piece down, he lets him put it back where it was and move a different one. He moves his king one space. The black queen takes a rook he hadn't noticed stood undefended. And now she stands looking at his king. He moves the king back. The black knight takes his bishop. All he has left are the king and queen and a handful of pawns. He moves the queen back to give her space to manoeuvre. Francis moves his knight and the king's life is at stake. The black queen comes across and slaughters a pawn. Thaddeus's king and queen stand backed into a corner, harassed by Francis's unpleasant queen, with no one left to defend them but two outlying pawns. Thaddeus hates this part of the game. He just wants it to finish now. He says so.

"Well, you've only got one more move before I slaughter you anyway," Francis points out. And Brother Thaddeus slowly understands this must be true.

This is actually one of Brother Thaddeus's better attempts. Too many evenings involve five mindless blunders countered by five swift responses from Francis and it's all over, leaving the prior thinking, *How could you be so stupid?* and politely saying, "Oh! Bad luck!"

✠   ✠   ✠

The dusk is well advanced. Bats flitter and swoop over the open expanse of the abbey court. High in the branches of the birch tree near the guesthouse, a blackbird was singing a few moments ago. The aromatic twilight distils the fragrance of grass and roses at the end of this warm day. The last light of the sun is almost off the horizon; but not yet – it's not dark yet, it's still today.

There's a bench in the abbey court, just next to the wide

archway of the entrance to the abbey precincts. It stands against the gatehouse wall, so if he has a quiet moment the porter can sit in the sun to say his rosary without abandoning his post. Right now Brother Martin is inside the porter's lodge, sorting out some letters that came in earlier for the abbot's attention, and packing up one or two parcels to be sent out. He should have done this earlier; he got involved in running errands between the checker and the guesthouse, then he has to admit he spent a long time chatting with one of the tenants from the row of cottages in the close. Now there's nothing for it but squinting in the candlelight, no certain way to get the best results in any task you care to name. Still, he wants to get all the rightful business of this day completed before the bell for Compline starts to ring.

But though Martin is fully occupied inside the porter's lodge, the amber glow of the candlelight spilling through the open door onto the dusty cobbles of the gateway, there is someone sitting on the bench just round the corner, as the colours drain from the sky and the shadows lengthen. You can't see much of him, clothed as he is in his black wool habit; only make out his dark form and the dusk-blurred pale contrast of his face and his folded hands. He's hardly drawing attention to himself, sitting quite motionless, silent, not even praying his rosary. He is praying, though, as it happens. Not the murmured repetition of carefully thought out compositions written by other people. Father Clement is praying the oldest and simplest, humblest prayer of all; just showing up and waiting. Like the father in Christ's own story kept watch for the prodigal son. Except there's no point in Father Clement climbing up onto a lookout post on the abbey walls; it's almost dark for one thing, and for another his eyesight is failing.

So he goes through no prophetic pantomime of climbing the watchtower; he keeps his vigil here, where he can't miss anyone coming home late through the postern door. He's on the verge of giving up. The day is ending. *Just a little while longer*, he thinks.

He can't quite disentangle his feelings. This lad who's wandered off has become for him an incarnation of hope; that the work can continue to the excellent standard they've striven to achieve, that the skills he possesses can be passed on to someone capable of using them while there is still time, that the last years of his life won't be a futile bleeding out of all he worked for, into the dust.

Where are you, lad? his heart whispers, though he does not speak. *Where are you? For God's sake, Brother Cedd, won't you come home?*

His whole body sags in sadness as the bell starts to toll for the men to gather. He can't bring himself to do as he should and get up without delay to make his way to the cloister. Stuck fast to his vigil, he can't bear to leave hope behind.

Then, striding across the court through the dusk comes his abbot, who sees him there and stops to say, "Are you all right, Father Clement?"

"Aye, Father, I am – I am. I was just... waiting." He gets slowly to his feet, all the sadness and weariness of the world there for the abbot to read in his face. He does his best to raise the ghost of a smile, and lets his feet that know the way through long familiarity take him across the court through the deepening shadows to the door of the church.

His abbot, meanwhile, steps briskly into the porter's lodge. "Would you mind," he asks Brother Martin, "hanging on here until Brother Thomas comes in? I expected him back by now. I've no doubt he'll be home any time soon. After that... well... I wonder if... could you leave the postern door unlocked until after Compline, please, Brother?" In response to the old-fashioned look this draws from Brother Martin, he says, "I doubt we'll be overrun by a swarm of thugs and robbers even if it's left unlocked the whole night. It's... oh, Brother Cedd's gone walkabouts and... if we could just have the door left unlocked. If it worries you, I'll spend the night here myself. I shan't sleep a wink if I'm lying abed wondering about him, thinking of him coming home only to find we've locked him out. I... please, Brother."

"Father John," says his porter good-naturedly, "you don't have to plead with me – you're my abbot! If it suits you to have all our cottagers and half the community murdered as they sleep, who am I to say no? Nay, go on – I'm only teasing you. I'll stay here until both your chicks are back under your wing, or until the morning comes; whichever comes soonest. It might surprise you to discover this, but I care about them too. On you go then – they'll be well sick of ringing that bell."

"Thank you," says John, relieved. "Thank you so much, Brother Martin."

"You are more than welcome. Oh – d'you want to take your letters with you? No? It'll do if I bring them over in the morning? Right you are then."

He's smiling as he turns back into the lodge. In Brother Martin's opinion, an abbot who cares about his lost sheep is the kind of shepherd you should be aiming for.

Chapter Twenty-Five

Silence, thinks Abbot John, should be at least relatively simple. Surely a proliferation of words must always complicate things, introduce muddle, and set hares running. Silence must be the ultimate simplicity. Language is fundamental to human relationship and society, and the renunciation of it – albeit partial – ought to make space in the soul. It should foster serenity. It should be like the speechless soaring arches of the abbey church rising into the shadows at Compline, losing themselves in friendly dark.

But there's nothing you can do to take the complication out of humanity. You can shut men up, but that won't necessarily quieten their souls. Not of itself.

He thinks of the men he has nursed in the infirmary, more than he can count by this time, and their loud, struggling silences. He remembers caring for Father Peregrine after the seizure took his speech – the intense, drawn-out misery and frustration. He thinks back on the day William took refuge with them after the fire, sitting in the infirmary clad in nothing but a towel for his modesty, tense and trembling, lips drawn back from his teeth in a grimace of pain, as John carefully washed the grit and soot and mud from the scrapes and burns. That big burn on his shoulder. Ouch. Silent ouch. He remembers the same man sitting in the choir during the time when everything had started to unravel, motionless, pale, tears flowing unchecked down his face. And, kneeling in Chapter before the community after the ship had gone down, trying to confess what he had done, but the words would not come. He could only prostrate himself. He couldn't speak. John had to tell them for him. But that mute prostration said everything.

Silence, he thinks, is by no means just nothing. Perhaps it is there to let what is real emerge; to suspend, for at least a little while, the brittle and the shallow. Like brushing dead leaves away from the place where clear water will come welling up from the body of the earth, if you give it a chance. If you don't choke it with a debris of words.

Love loves silence. Still tugging at his conscience is his own silence in the refectory at the midday meal yesterday. He could not bring himself to throw that poor lad into confusion by stopping the reading, drawing attention to the error, making him say the sentence again. Already the boy was stammering, his knees shaking, his hands trembling as he turned the heavy page. It was his first time. Silence clothes with compassion the humiliation of small mistakes, refraining from tearing away every shred of ambiguity to expose them. Silence gives dignity to our frailty. Yet some of the custumals he studied at Cambridge, in preparation to take up the abbacy, made it plain the abbot is recommended to stop the reader, point out the mistake. What for, he wonders. To humble him? To break his pride? To foster a lowly and teachable spirit? The documents didn't say. All that, probably. So maybe he was wrong to choose the gentle alternative of silently letting it pass. Who knows? Every single day brings questions he cannot answer, choices he cannot be sure are wise or sound.

Right now, he's glad Theo is handling Collatio for him. Just at the moment his heart is too full to want to speak. Even more than he worries whether he did the right thing with Colin in the refectory, he searches his conscience again and again for some clue to how he might better have watched over their missing novice. Has he been too strict? Too negligent? Too preoccupied? Were there signs of turmoil or unhappiness he should have detected? What went wrong? He so hoped Brother Cedd would come back to them, but those hopes are wearing thin by this hour of the day. He imagined the young man coming to find him in the abbot's lodge after Vespers, admitting his misgivings had caused him to waver but he'd had second thoughts. But now it is nearly time for Compline, and still no sign of him. Brother Cedd... a quiet, reticent boy. Not aloof, just lacking in confidence. He gave no indication of being so burdened he had to drop it all and leave. He must have done what seemed admirable to him – borne it in silence. If he'd listened to the reading of the Rule, he'd have grasped there is a time to speak; to trust his abbot enough to confide his apprehension and the faltering of his faith. Silence is a beautiful thing, but it's not always a good idea.

By now, the community is gathered in this place alongside the chapel, the north walk of the cloister, for Collatio. How spacious, but how intimate – brotherly, indeed – is this silent coming together. John closes his eyes and in silence his soul reaches into the disciplined stillness of this family of brothers, this house of men who have each offered his whole life, one by one. To touch the hem of Christ's robe. To abandon himself without reserve to the loving mystery of God in holy silence.

And when Theodore opens the book on the lectern there in the cloister, finding the place with his finger and beginning to read, the extract from John Cassian's writings is about the perils of silence. *How odd*, thinks John, as he listens.

Cassian is warning of how silence can be misused. How a monk can fancy himself patient and forbearing because he has said nothing, when the cold look and sullen attitude say it all for him. Like a man who protested he didn't push someone who is blind into the ditch. And he may not have done, but if he stood and looked on while the blind man stumbled and fell in, how is that better? Theo reads the part where Cassian writes of Judas Iscariot, in Gethsemane, identifying his Lord for the angry mob, singling him out with the wordless, lethal gesture of a kiss. *This*, thinks the abbot, *is so depressing*. The passage ends, pointing out how deep is the grief when somebody you trusted turns you in.

And the words hang on the air like a breath of frost, a gravebreath. Silence that pretended to be love, nothing more than a betrayal. It leaves a taste in the mouth of bitterest disappointment.

Thanks, John Cassian. Thanks, Theo. Thanks, Lord, he thinks, bitterly. The community receive the words in breathing, heartbeating silence; the abbot does what he can to feel his way to anything good.

Father Theodore adds words of his own. Listening to him, John catches sadness in his voice. Theo, too, is mourning the loss of his straying lamb.

"The silence to which we are called, brothers, is more than mere refraining from words. I mean, it's something better than accusations or complaints unspoken. It's receptive, understanding. Silence that sees and forgives. Companionable. Loving. Warm. So that when he is with us, a man would feel he has come home."

John looks up, hearing the small sounds of movement, to see Brother Conradus treading cautiously into their midst from the kitchen buildings, along the east walk. He's going softly, stepping light, taking care to disturb the time of reflection as little as he can. When he reaches the assembled community, he so positions himself as to catch the abbot's eye, among the monks with their cowled heads, their hands folded into their wide sleeves. John watches him.

Brother Conradus looks very directly at his abbot and lifts his right hand, extending the forefinger and middle finger just behind his ear, his thumb and other fingers pressed into his palm. This is a word from the monastic sign language of the silence:

"novice". He lowers his hand, pauses, then lifts it again, this time in a repeated motion of the first three fingers towards his mouth, to denote eating. He lowers his hand. With the slightest smile, discreetly, he now moves his fingers, a little curved, fluttering upward, like a ripple of wings: "Hallelujah". His eyes still fixed on his abbot, he nods. Then his hands come to rest. He tucks them into his wide, black sleeves. He bends his head.

Abbot John feels joy spreading through his whole being like the warm headiness of wine. Hoping Father Theodore has also seen, he glances across to his novice master, just in time to catch the luminous radiance of the biggest grin on Theo's face in the moment before recollecting himself to impassivity as he steps away from the lectern.

The abbot closes his eyes. Thank you, he whispers in the silence of his heart. Thank you.

As the community forms up to process into the choir for Compline, before they set off, the abbot pushes through to Father Clement's side. "Brother Cedd is home," he murmurs in his ear. Relief so sudden and sharp it is almost like pain. As the old man turns his head in a quick glance of grateful acknowledgment, the abbot sees there are tears in his dim blue, bleary eyes.

✠   ✠   ✠

"Compline bell," remarks Brother Tom, wiping his mouth and hands free of grease on the big linen napkin. "By heck, that was good. Brother Conradus must be pleased to see us home. Worth coming back for, eh? Have you had enough?"

Two hearty suppers have awaited them on their return, covered in dampened cloths so the food won't dry out. They've already eaten with Madeleine and William, but after the long journey, what they had at Caldbeck recedes into the past. An egg for each of them, bread from today's baking with some fresh butter and a modest wedge of cheese with a generous dollop of spicy plum preserve. Really good cheese; creamy, with a sharp, full, tangy flavour and little salt crystals within it. A handful of crisp herb salad, a bowl of apples and a jug of ale. The kitchener ushers them into his domain with a smiling welcome. He's laid two places for them at the big work table where the servers and readers eat. He looks unsurprised to see Brother Cedd and makes no comment on his absence at all. Neither did Brother Martin in the porter's lodge when he came out to admit them. Conradus uncovers the food for them, fetches the ale jug, and pours a big mugful for each of them, then leaves them to their supper.

Brother Tom polishes off his second supper with appreciation. Truth be told, though he accepts gratefully the food Brother Conradus gives him, Brother Cedd struggles to eat it. Apprehension about what comes next makes him feel a bit sick.

"I'm not sure what to do." He looks to Brother Tom for his advice. "Am I just meant to go into Compline as if nothing had happened, and then go to bed in the usual way?"

Tom, picking a bit of sorrel from between his teeth, considers this question.

"Father John will know you're back," he says. "I don't think he'll wait until the morning; he'll want to see you after Compline, silence or not. I suggest you come into chapel with me – just as you said, as if nothing has happened – then wait at the end until everyone else has gone. My guess is that Father Abbot will do the same. If I were you, I think what I'd do next is go and kneel by his stall and see what he says. He'll tell you what he wants you to do – which will be either go back to his house with him to let him know what's been happening in your addle-pated head, or else he'll ask you to come and explain yourself in the morning after Chapter."

Tom contemplates the novice, who looks shivery and scared. "You don't need to be afraid of Father John. He looks a bit grim at times, I know, but he's kind. He's seen all possible permutations of doubt and despair in the infirmary. He's on your side; he's not interested in punishment or humiliation. Besides which, he's had too many struggles of his own to think badly of yours. He's a man you can trust, is our abbot. He'll help you get to the root of things, put your finger on what's important. Don't be frightened of him. He'll have spent this entire day grieving over you, wondering whether or not you are coming home. He won't be angry."

"Grieving over… really? Over *me*?" Brother Cedd gapes at Tom, incredulous.

"Over you. Yes. Really. I'd put money on it. Well now, I should say they've been ringing that bell long enough. No need to ruffle the abbot's feathers by coming in late. Shall we go? Take our plates to the scullery, there's a good lad. I'll just cover this ale and put it away, and the butter."

Chapter Twenty-Six

The abbot gives the knock, and with a supple, subdued ripple of robes, as one body the community rises.

"*Iube, Dómine, benedícere.*"[25]

The sun has set, and the steady warmth of candlelight shines on the huge shared breviaries set upon the slanting lecterns.

The response comes back: "*Noctem quiétam et finem perféctum concédat nobis Dóminus omnípotens.*[26] *Amen.*"

Brother Cedd, embarrassed, his head bowed, feeling conspicuous, has taken his usual place among the other novices. He stumbled on Brother Cassian's foot as he went past him, and Cassian put out a hand to steady him.

The familiar prayers unfold in peace; the short reading, the versicle and response, the silent examination of conscience, the Lord's Prayer, the confession and absolution, more responses. Then the psalms, back and forth across the chapel like the tidal rhythm of the sea on a calm night; unhurried, blessed by darkness, by shadows, by the friendliness of long acquaintance.

In the monastic way of things, they alternate verses; and each verse is punctuated by a little firebreak of silence. It makes nonsense of the text, but it keeps a man awake for that very reason. Without that small break, it is so easy for the mouth to be left praying while the mind wanders off.

---

25 "Pray, sir, a blessing."
26 "May the Lord Almighty grant a quiet night and a perfect end."

"*Qui hábitat in adiutório Altíssimi*",[27] begins Psalm 90 – and the cantor pauses – then finishes the verse: "*in protectióne Dei cæli commorábitur.*"[28]

The quiet sea of the chanting voices flows in their turn: "*Dicet Dómino: Suscéptor meus es tu, et refúgium meum...*"[29] and pauses. Then takes up the chant again: "*Deus meus sperábo in eum.*"[30]

Brother Cedd loves Compline. Its serenity is imbued with unshakeable confidence, the peace of the soul whose trust is in God. He hopes Father Gilbert never manages to infiltrate the Office with polyphony; and notes that even thinking it tells him he imagines his own future is here.

As he participates in the cadences of the chant, he is conscious of the community as one living being, against whose side he can lean, can rest. The common purpose of prayer weaves a net of integrated intention that upholds him. He experiences it afresh, having questioned his place in it, and acknowledges how rare such a thing must be.

He wonders what on earth he's going to say to the abbot, how he can possibly give an account of himself. Still the sense of uselessness and inadequacy wants to push him into absolute despair. Among the fine scholars and accomplished men in this abbey, what has he to offer that's of any worth at all? How can he make any kind of contribution, or find a role for himself that will be of service to anyone?

At the same time, as he looks at the peaceful faces of his community, illumined by candlelight and also by the serious joy of this calling, he wants so much to be part of it.

Then, quite apart from that, transcending the exterior detail of his life and theirs, the extraordinary experience in the apple loft, the opening of his heart to receive Christ's presence. *How can this*

---

27 "Whosoever dwells in the shelter of the Most High..."
28 "Abides under the protection of the God of heaven."
29 "He shall say to the Lord, thou art my stronghold and refuge..."
30 "My God, in whom I trust."

sit alongside the Eucharist? he puzzles. *Is there more than one way to receive the living reality of Christ?*

He tries to remember what Father Theodore has taught them, about touching Christ the living Word in the Scriptures and in the tradition of Holy Church. He feels sure Father Abbot has spoken to them many times about kindness and gentleness as a sort of Eucharistic grace... "*Remember me*", the words of Jesus, and also of the thief on the cross. And now he can't recall what it was Father John said.

But he does remember with absolute clarity William saying that all anybody has to do is humbly ask, and then Christ will come in. And he knows he is not the same now as before he said his "Amen" to William's prayer. He doesn't feel excited or joyous, nothing like that. Just this unlikely and entirely unfamiliar assurance deep inside, that despite his apprehension about facing Abbot John, and his conviction that he has nothing worthwhile to offer this community, somehow, regardless of the outcome, everything will be all right.

Then they are singing the *Salve Regina*, the Office is ended, they are in silence now. He does as Brother Thomas told him, stays in his place as the community quietly disperses. He sits with his eyes closed, listening to the discreet sounds of community movement: robes, sandals, the creak of wood. He feels men walking all around him, the subdued stir of their going.

The unexpectedness of a hand laid on his shoulder startles open his eyes. He looks round, and there's Father Theodore, not wanting to walk away without the "Welcome home" of a touch, a nod, and a smile. He loves Father Theodore. They all do. And he knows the solemns call him just "Theo". With a pang of insecurity, he wonders, how do you come to be so loved? Can it really be only by staying? Is a man's own self honestly all that is asked? Is it enough?

Nobody else looks at him; they are in the Great Silence

now Compline is ended, and part of the silence is solitude, the withdrawal from seeking involvement and interaction. The treasure of the silence is the unadulterated company of God. In a community, this can be given only by common permission; you have to leave people alone. Brother Cedd knows that; but he's grateful that Colin the postulant risks a glance and a quick smile as he goes by. He wonders if Colin has noticed he's been away all day. Of course he has. What does he think about it, then? Does he care? Do any of them? Will it make a difference if he goes or if he stays, to anybody at all except himself?

Often after Compline, here and there in the chapel a man will stay on in his own private prayer. Not tonight. Brother Cedd, watching the chapel decisively empty, realizes that every man here understands the situation completely, and is withdrawing from intruding on what comes next.

Father Bernard, last to go, walks round the choir extinguishing the lights – all except the lamp where Brother Cedd is sitting, the light near the way out, Abbot John's, and those of the two stalls nearest his. The sacristan puts the snuffer back in its place, and unobtrusively walks away; but he sets the lighted lantern down on the floor nearest the candle by the door. You think of others. This has been drilled into all of them by Father Theodore since the day they crossed the threshold. You are realistic about your own needs – don't starve yourself, don't beat yourself silly, don't torture yourself with misery unshared – but you think of others, always, every time. *Like that,* thinks Cedd; *you think it through. You leave them a lantern. That's how they know you care about them. You leave them a light. You don't take it with you.* Maybe that's the only kind of contribution they want of him. He hopes so, because he surely can't think of anything better he could have to give.

Now this is it, then. Across the choir, his abbot is sitting perfectly still, not looking at him, but obviously waiting. With that horrible sinking feeling in the pit of his stomach, Brother

Cedd wonders how much trouble he's going to be in. Time to find out. As he crosses over the flagged divide between the two facing sets of stalls, he wonders if Abbot John will actually tell him he can't stay now. That you can't just wander off for a day. Or maybe extend his novitiate for months and months if he doesn't just tell him to pack his things and go in the morning. Or perhaps there will be a scolding, taking him to task, reminding him to confess it at tomorrow's Chapter, asking him who he thinks he is to be taking matters into his own hands like this.

Brother Cedd kneels by the entrance to the abbot's stall, in the pool of candlelight, getting the words ready in his mind – *I implore you, Father…* or maybe, *Father, I do not deserve…*

"Hello," says Father John, with simple friendliness. "I can't tell you how glad I am to see you safe back. Are you all right?"

Brother Cedd didn't know what to expect, but not that, anyway. To be spoken to like a friend. He lifts his head, and meets the abbot's gaze. The man looks happy, genuinely pleased to see him.

Father John gets up from his place in the abbot's stall, and steps down to the stone-flagged way where Cedd is kneeling. "Budge up," he says unaffectedly. "Make room for me."

He sits on the floor beside him, leaning his back against the wood panelling that fronts the stalls. Brother Cedd, disconcerted, abandons his humble kneeling and does the same.

"What happened?" John asks him gently.

And it all comes tumbling out. The wretched inadequacy of his dull ordinariness. Bad at Latin, worse at Greek, only just able to sight-read. Can't follow some of Father Theodore's explanations of theology and philosophy. Bored out of his skull by some of the books they have to read. Not really sure how to go about his hours of private prayer – what you should do, what you should say. Nothing mystical happens. And then (now he really hadn't meant to mention this, it just comes out somehow) some of the brothers drive him to distraction, irritate him beyond belief. Brother Cassian whistling absently through his teeth, Brother Felix always – always – having to be first, having to be right, taking Cedd's ideas expressed tentatively in privacy and waving them about as if they were his own. Brother Boniface sitting next to him in chapel, sliding the notes like a man paid to sing slushy love songs in a tavern. Brother Robert – oh, save us – Brother Robert! Anything you say to him, anything at all, if there are two possible ways to understand a thing, you can guarantee, every time without exception he'll take it the way you don't mean, however far-fetched and unlikely that interpretation might be. How can a man so thick be so inventive?

He stops abruptly. Criticizing the brethren like this is absolutely forbidden. You speak directly or you don't speak at all. His own sense of inferiority might at least have made his abbot feel sorry for him, like a dog that grovels at your feet hopes not to be kicked. But what is coming out of his mouth now strikes him as sheer sneering spite. And he feels ashamed.

Slowly, in the silence that follows this outpouring, he makes himself look at his abbot to see how it is received. John is sitting, his head tipped back, leaning against the stalls, the biggest grin imaginable on his face as he listens to this.

"Oh, my brother," he says, "you do me good. You sound exactly like me. Ashes in your teeth, isn't it, sometimes?" He pauses. Then he says, still without looking at the novice: "And is that all it was? For this you wanted to leave us? Did you truly think anybody else was any different?"

"Well…" Brother Cedd struggles for an answer that doesn't sound too hopelessly lame. "Everybody else is so patient, so accomplished, so kind. Apart from me."

The abbot is laughing now, shaking his head. "Thinks every single man of us!" he says.

"Really?" Brother Cedd feels inclined to push this. He

recognizes that such a conversation may not too often be possible. Self-preoccupation is wearisome in other people. He will probably have to shut up about this now if he stays; but it frets at him all the time.

"I watch the professed brothers sometimes, here in the chapel. They don't look ill at ease – well, mostly. They look serene and composed, as though they have it all together, as though they've got the hang of it in a way I don't think I ever will. That's why I went to find Father William. Because he was the only man I ever saw sitting in chapel with tears running down his face. I thought he'd understand."

The abbot looks at him then, taken aback. "William? De Bulmer? My brother-in-law? Is that where you've been? How did you know where he lives?"

Brother Cedd feels his face grow hot with embarrassment. "I'm sorry, Father. I shouldn't have been listening," he confesses. "Back in May when the bishop was here, Father William was up in the novitiate talking with Father Theodore, and saying something about his house in Caldbeck. My family lives near Caldbeck, so I knew where he meant. There was only one place it could be, because I knew all the other families settled there. I thought if I found him, he'd understand what it's like to feel so out of step, so confoundedly miserable."

"I see," says the abbot. "And did he?"

Brother Cedd hesitates. "He… well, he didn't seem all that keen to talk about his own experiences. He said life is mostly about ordinary things – just the daily round and the work we do. He said nobody can ever live up to expectations. That if I found anything lacking in the community I should put it there myself, and that could be my contribution. And he said… well… I think 'sulkiness', 'petulance', and 'self-pity' were the words he used."

The abbot digests this in silence. "That… erm… that doesn't

sound so very understanding," he says then. "Not what you'd been hoping for, I'd guess. Was that… it sounds as if it could have been extremely hurtful."

"I know." Brother Cedd nods. "Doesn't it! But somehow, it wasn't. There's something about him, that man. He's quite frightening in a way, and not very approachable. And, yes, he didn't pull his punches. But that wasn't the main thing, Father."

John waits.

"He said… that the whole point of life is coming to know Jesus – to actually meet him, he said. Live every day with him. He meant, be with him like you and I are sitting here together now. He said all I had to do was ask, and that would happen."

He lapses into silence. John takes this in, asks: "And – did you?"

"I wasn't sure how to, or what to say. I asked if he'd say the prayer for me, so I could just say the Amen. And he did. Just talking to Jesus as if he was really there with us, up in the apple loft! And, Father… I can hardly put this into words, it seems so personal – but when he did that, when he spoke to Jesus I mean, his voice was so full of love and trust. It brought out into the open the thing that made me want to go and find him, though I couldn't have put my finger on it before I heard him make that prayer. It's partly because one way and another you can see he's been through the mill, but it's also that hidden thing inside him… I'm not sure what to call it… but the thing it most reminded me of is love. I think it somehow makes him into a living link to Jesus. I can't put it any better than that. But that prayer of his – I did say 'Amen', and it has made a difference inside me."

Both men feel the quality of silence undergo a subtle shift. This happens sometimes. Silence becomes presence, something holy, a place you don't want to leave and don't easily forget. Holy ground. The abbot closes his eyes. *Thank you, William. Thank you, Jesus.*

Then he brings himself back to the question he must ask. "So. What do you want to do? Things got bad enough that you had to take some time out. That's all right. I understand. What do you want to do now?"

Brother Cedd swallows. "Well, I'd better explain myself to Father Theodore in the morning. And I'm very sorry I just walked off without saying anything. But will it be all right if... can I just come home, and carry on?"

The abbot nodded. "You can indeed. If 'home' is what it is to you, then here is where you should be. And, Brother Cedd, I don't want to put any kind of unhelpful burden onto you, but I think you ought to know, you are not the only man here to feel inadequate. This day long I have been asking myself what kind of a useless abbot must I be that you couldn't come and talk to me, and I know Father Theodore has been worried to death about you. And Father Clement, sitting outside in the dusk near the porter's lodge all this evening, waiting – do you not know how much he depends on you? Haven't you realized how vital to him is your skill in lettering and illumination, now his sight is fading? I think it just about tore him in two when he saw that you'd gone. It's been a long day for him."

Brother Cedd looks at the abbot, shocked. "But... my work in the scriptorium is nothing special! Anybody could do it."

"Oh, aye, of course," says the abbot, getting up, reaching out his hand to Brother Cedd to pull him onto his feet: "but that's not what Father Clement says. Still, what would he know? Come on, lad, it's getting late now. Time for bed."

Cupping his hand round the candles near his stall and then Cedd's, he blows them out. Father Bernard wouldn't let that pass, thinks the novice. "Always snuff, lads; never blow." Still, at least the abbot does pinch out the smouldering spark at the top of each wick before he leaves it.

As they reach the archway through to the south transept and

the night stairs, the abbot blows out the last candle, stoops, and picks up the lantern. But then he pauses. Brother Cedd looks at him in enquiry. When John meets the young man's gaze, his eyes are very serious. "Brother Cedd, I'm in two minds whether to mention this. What I'm about to tell you now is a great trust. You must never pass it on, not to anybody. Do you understand me?"

Cedd nods, round-eyed, wondering what on earth this can be.

"My brother-in-law, William de Bulmer – it is of utmost importance that we be discreet about where he lives. I don't know if word reached you of this, but during the time he lived as part of this community, he attempted to take his own life."

Brother Cedd feels this information jar through his whole being in brutal shocks. John, holding the lantern, sees it in his face. "Oh. You didn't know. Maybe I should not have told you. Never mind."

That image flashes back in Cedd's mind again as if it were playing out before him right here and now; the white, strained, exhausted face, and the tears rolling down unchecked. Tried to take his own life. Whatever happened?

"The thing is," the abbot continues, "as I expect you realize, that is a felony; and by some unfortunate mishap – we do not know how – the bishop got wind of it. For one reason and another he has a very low opinion of my brother-in-law. He has tried quite hard to track him down. So, though William comes and goes, we are discreet; we do not discuss who he is or where he lives. And we are vague about his personal history, if asked. His life depends on it, do you see? Please don't tell anyone – apart from Father Theodore, who also knows where he is. Don't let it be known where you went, or to whom. Just keep it close, keep it safe. Brother – can I trust you? I do hope so."

"I will never tell anyone but Father Theodore, upon my life," the novice promises soberly: "ever."

Father John looks at him carefully, and nods. "Thank you,"

he says as they come to the bottom of the stairs: "because I love that man. He is very dear to me. He's not easy company, but you couldn't wish for a stauncher friend. In any time of trouble, he's like a rock. I'm glad you found your way to him. He gave you good advice."

He is speaking one shade above silence. They must not violate the holy peace of the night with conversation. The abbot gives the lantern into Cedd's hand so he can see to climb the stairs. The moon lights his own way along the cloister to the abbot's lodge.

Chapter Twenty-Seven

"Did the day go well?" asks Madeleine, as she gets down the linen bag with her spindle and carders, pulls out the big sack of fleece from behind the chair. "It was good of Brother Thomas to bring us down those sacks of grain and clothing – well, good of my brother to send him with them, I suppose. He just does as he's told. Still, it was kind and a big help that he fixed the scythe and sorted out the fence for us. And I think you got quite a bit more fruit picked, you and Brother Cedd, didn't you?"

"Aye, I think it went well," says her husband. "I hope so anyway. I hope that lad doesn't give up on the path he's taken. It's always such a sadness when someone leaves."

She laughs. "What? If that isn't the pot calling the kettle black, I don't know what is! Surely, if it's not the right thing for a man to stay then it must be the right thing to leave. What matters is not if he goes or stays but if he comes to know his own soul, follows his guiding star, is true to the voice of his heart."

"Aye," he says. "Of course," he adds. By the tone of his voice and the aversion of his face, Madeleine knows she's annoyed him now. She tries to make it better.

"While I was picking the blackberries along the hedgerow, I saw you took the baskets of apples up with the lad to the big loft, and you were there ages. Did he tell you something of his trouble, when you had that moment to yourselves?"

"Aye, he did."

She waits to hear what that trouble might have been, but evidently he's not going to tell her; so she probes further, curious: "Did he say what it was made him decide to come here?"

"Aye. He did."

"So – why then?"

Shadowed in the shadows his eyes meet hers. She can't see his face properly, his back is to the window, his face is obscured in the dusky failing light. But she can feel the tension of his reluctance to tell her. Why? She's his wife – wouldn't he want to share it with her, talk it through?

With a quick sigh of impatience, he says: "Apparently, him sitting on the other side of the choir from me at St Alcuin's, he had opportunity to see tears flow that I could not help. So he thought I'd understand. That's what he said."

And now he has her absolute fixed attention. "Tears? About what?"

"Oh, heaven! Madeleine, surely you know! About you, about lying to John, about the mess I made of the money and the whole damned tangle I got myself into. It all about tore me to shreds. Some days it was too much for me."

"So you would sit in chapel weeping, in the Office?"

"Sometimes. Not too often, I hope."

"And nobody saw? No one cared or did anything about it?"

"Madeleine, what could they do? How could I have told anyone about you and me? And what was to be done about the money except for them to pull their belts in and make the best of it? They didn't berate me or beat me; they understood. And tears aren't especially uncommon in a monastery. There's much that's difficult to swallow and precious little privacy. You can't always keep it back until you're alone in your cell."

"Oh. So – what was it Brother Cedd thought you'd understand? What's he done?"

"He hasn't done anything, he's just struggling."

"With what?"

"Oh, great God in heaven give me patience – you don't give up, do you? Why don't you mind your own business? Just leave it alone!"

"William, that's really rude –"

"*Rude?* I'm rude? Not you're over-inquisitive, poking about in what's not yours to know?"

"What? That's so mean! Why do you have to be so touchy? What's the matter with you? Get over yourself!"

He draws breath to reply, then he stops, completely, standing absolutely still. Madeleine is familiar with this by now, but not sure she will ever get used to it. She has realized it is part of what it means to share a life with a man thirty years a monk. At first when she saw him do this, she thought he was overcome by anger – that's what's usually happening, in her experience, with people who stop dead and stand in total silence when you criticize them. Mostly, it means trouble brewing; they are fomenting outrage. But not, she has learned, with this man. It *is* about anger, but he is not getting ready to let fly. She knows what his silence means now. It's the time it takes to humble himself, rein in his natural responses of defensiveness, cancel the instinct to a sharp retort. These short silences are her windows into his self-mastery, and she has learned to esteem them, give him time, not assume he's holding out on her and get ready for a fight. Neither does she try to intervene with physical closeness – a hug, an apology, an endearment. She knows (*now* – she didn't at first) it's all he can do to cope with himself in these moments; he's already trying his very best and has nothing left over for cuddles.

So she waits. And, quietly, as he always does, he apologizes. "I am so sorry, Madeleine. I was disrespectful and churlish in what I said. I humbly ask your forgiveness."

And although what fits right in with monastic life sounds

almighty strange in an ordinary household, in this cottage, she thinks every time he does it, *Oh, I love this man*.

She knows, because he's told her about it, that these few moments of struggle it takes him to find the self-control he needs, have made trouble for him his whole life long; not as a monk only, but as a child as well. What they wanted – his father, his mother, his novice master, his prior – was absolute immediate obedience: in his attitude, in his demeanour, in his face; not in his words and actions only. There was no "as soon as you're ready" about it; they meant "*now*".

Those few unresponsive seconds, they have got him thrashed times past counting; but he can't seem to get it down to "now", no matter how hard he tries. It just takes him a moment to get past the black fury, the red rage, wanting to have the upper hand when someone admonishes him. It's not that he believes himself to be always in the right, but too many years living under excoriating injustice and mocking cruelty make it hard to live with any kind of reprimand. It makes him flare up inside, it burns, snarls. And it does take those few short seconds to control it.

It isn't fear that returns him every time to this habit of self-discipline, this stilling silence. The regimes he lived under drove him beyond fear. The child who lives each day with fear becomes simply used to being frightened all the time. It is a given, and no longer determines choices and actions. It's very hard to dominate someone who is habitually afraid. Anything new comes too late to frighten him. He's scared already, and what he does will make no difference to that. The man who is always afraid will dare and imperil anything, unable to evaluate risk in a life already terrifying.

He persists with his obstinate effort to get self-mastery down to a perfect art. In part he does so for shame – he feels bad that he can't immediately achieve it, that this rage always boils over inside. But it's also simply habit; it has become reflexive, to stop, to breathe, to wait, to get himself under control. It is the discipline of a lifetime. More compellingly, a long time ago he learned contempt of violence; and he cannot bear to see it. Cruelty and pain, screaming terror – they sicken him to his stomach. He cannot stand it. Even thinking of the slaughter of a pig, an ox, makes him vomit. He can only just cope with Madeleine breaking the neck of a pot-boiler.

When they go to the market – she is used to this now, but couldn't understand what was happening at first – if, as so often happens, he sees a child sobbing, broken-hearted, pleading in futile desperation with an indifferent parent; bawled at, flung aside, lambasted with words, with sticks, with whatever comes to hand, for some misdemeanour; he has to walk away. Right then, even if he's in the middle of haggling for a price, regardless of who is saying what to him. He can't blot it out. He says it interferes with his eyesight – for a moment he can't see, so wild is the sorrow and despair it sets off inside him.

And he tells her that for the greater part of his life he tried to fight back, to become somehow invincible – more ruthless, colder, crueller than anything that threatened him. But then came his curious encounter with Christ, with love, with kindness; and the deeper reality broke through – the truth is that he just hates it, this violence which never stops, this endless bullying, the calling card of the human race. So far as it lies with him, he will no longer inhabit the same space. What he has no power to put a stop to, he will leave.

But he has to live with the unpalatable reality that the seeds of it are buried in the recesses of his soul; they sprout, they send out shoots. Despite his best efforts he can't weed it out, shake it off. All he can do is decide how to deal with it. And that takes a few moments of silence. When he stops like that, becomes quite still, he is not praying, he tells her; in those moments he is beyond praying, though he is striving for faithfulness. He says he has to trust Christ to hold on to him then, while he lets go of everything and allows the rage to subside.

And so here he stands, in the dusk, in this now comfortably familiar room. It's time to light the candles. Outside, already, a hunting owl is calling. The moon is rising. He achieves containment, and manages to say it – "I am so sorry, Madeleine. I was disrespectful and churlish in what I said. I humbly ask your forgiveness."

And though it inspires in her this upsurge of love, at the same time there's something about the terrible control of it that makes her feel hemmed in, as if she can hardly breathe. And then it's as though the words speak themselves without her bidding: "Oh, for heaven's sake, William! Don't take yourself so seriously – it's not as bad as that!"

Even as she says it, she is already thinking, *Why do I always say something like this? It only winds him up even more.* She looks for, and sees, the tic in his face, the clench in his jaw. This is usually the point when the trap springs, a net of tense silence closing around them for the rest of the evening. In silence they finish the day, go to bed without speaking, and in the end she reaches for his hand in the dark as they lie in bed without moving, without speaking. Apart from anything else, it's intensely irritating and makes the day end very late.

Something in her suddenly decides the pattern cannot be inevitable. She moves to stand in front of him. She gives him a little space, stands more than a yard from him, waiting respectfully until his gaze meets hers. Still that tic, that flexing jaw muscle. His eyes hold her gaze but she sees his reluctance, how intolerable it is to have to face her standing there.

"William," she says, quietly, but not trying to appease him. Nothing wheedling or beseeching, just speaking his name. "Please. It's me. You married me. You love me. I didn't mean to belittle you or hurt you. I did not intend contempt or disparagement. It's just how I am; I spoke too hasty like I always do. Please, dearest friend, can you manage to put it down, let it go? I know how much people have abused and humiliated you. I know how the rage inside you goes wild. But we don't have to do this. I think you have the courage and humility to see past my rough clumsiness and know that I don't mean to slight you. And I didn't realize I was being intrusive; I was only interested. I thought it would be all right for a man to share such things with his wife. I mean, I'd tell you anything. I... oh, William, what I'm saying is, can't you... no... please will you forgive me for getting it wrong?"

And she realizes, that last thing she says – the simple request for forgiveness, without excuses or defensiveness – is what he needs. He knows how to respond to it. It belongs to his lifelong practice of the monastic way. He doesn't know how to find his way through the tangle of the most ordinary human interaction, but he knows the pattern of seeking and granting forgiveness as a method of beginning again.

In the gathering dusk, he nods. "Of course," he says: and suddenly sees the funny side of it himself. The tension goes out of him with a sigh and he runs his hand over his head. "What am I like?"

She steps forward then, and takes him into her arms.

"Does nothing change?" he whispers into her hair. "Does nothing ever change? Am I never going to conquer this? I *am* touchy; you're quite right."

"Sweetheart," she says, "you don't have to be so hard on yourself. I love you more than I know how to tell you, and you're doing fine."

He holds her, so close, so tender, so dearly enfolded. As if he would never, never let her go.

But for all it is so intimate, so beautiful, she knows he'll still never tell her. Whatever Brother Cedd confided in him will be safe for eternity.

Chapter Twenty-Eight

The day the abbot informed Colin that the community had accepted him as a postulant, he thought his heart would hardly contain the excitement and pride. Up until that point, his accommodation was in the guesthouse, his meetings with Father Theodore were in the small parlour in the west range, and the only other part of the cloister he'd been into was the abbot's house. He'd been in the church, of course, but only the nave. He hadn't gone beyond the parish side of the altar.

Tonight, as darkness falls, he thinks back on that day, reliving it vividly. Abbot John had explained everything to him, how the next morning he would come before the community at Chapter to beg admittance. There he must prostrate himself, asking to be received. The abbot had assured him it was not that there was any doubt about him – they'd already been asked and said yes – but this was the procedure to follow. He floated through that day, and yet it seemed like a lifetime. Through the night he hardly slept a wink. In the morning, so excited he felt sick, he had waited nervously in the guesthouse until the bell rang for the morrow Mass. There in the church, Father Theodore had come to find him after the blessing at the end, and led him through to the chapter house, and there the adventure had begun.

Once admitted, the novices took charge of him, taking him with them at the point they left the Chapter meeting, showing him the novitiate room where they had their teaching circle. Looking back tonight, he lingers on that memory. He remembers it so clearly, walking in through the door for the first time; the comfortable, pervasive smell of woodsmoke, the study desks and shelves stacked with books, the circle of low benches and stools, the statue of St Benedict over in the corner, the crucifix up on the wall, the morning sun shining in to fill the room with light.

Not that they'd let him stand gazing long. They wanted to show him his cell. It was next to Brother Cedd's. It didn't need much of a tour. Rectangular, small, plain, it had a lancet window set too high in the wall to see out. There was a low, narrow bed of basic plank frame, with linen sheets and a wool blanket – and, he would later discover, a straw mattress like those favoured by the poor. On the whitewashed wall, above the prie-dieu against the wall opposite the bed, a crucifix hung on a nail. A basic nightstand stood beside the bed, and Brother Cassian lifted aside its small linen curtain to show him the pot inside for night-time use. Cassian also pulled the scourge out from beneath the bed for him to see, then pushed it back with his foot saying, with a grin, "But not yet. Make up your mind about the life before you start belabouring yourself. Don't go wild."

Other than that, a wooden chest of modest size was provided for storing his clothes, a hook on the door for his cloak and, against the wall below the window, a stool and table of practical size so he could study. The floor was of bare, scrubbed boards.

To some men, so small, austere a room seemed dauntingly penitential. To Colin, who had never had his own room and had to share a bed with his brother, it felt like giddy luxury. He wondered if he might be lonely there all night by himself; and thought, on balance, no.

And that is how it began. He has been very tired, sometimes, in these first few weeks – so much to learn and remember, so much to get wrong. But the friendly hands of the novices steer him to where he should be. Brother Cedd, especially, he has appreciated. A quiet, unassuming lad, sleeping in the next cell, they have emerged together often. In silence of course, but it has surprised Colin to discover the extent to which warmth and kindness can be expressed without words, and how close it is possible to feel to someone without needing lengthy conversation.

Tonight, he leaves the church, briefly visits the reredorter, then ascends the stairs to the cells. From his own cell he fetches his candle and lights it from one of those burning in the hallway just nearby. Brother Robert made this sturdy holder for it, here in the abbey's pottery – he knows; Robert pointed it out and told him so, with some pride. It's a bit wonky, but not a bad effort for a novice potter.

Once he's been clothed, he will sleep in his habit, setting aside his scapular, belt, and cowl. He gets into the feel of it now, in these weeks of preparation, wearing his undershirt and tunic, taking off his hose and shoes and belt. He kneels down to pray at the prie-dieu, then climbs into bed. He can extinguish the candle, because he won't have to get up for Nocturns until he's clothed as a novice. After that, he'll have to leave it burning so he can see what he's doing when the sacristan wakes them for Matins. That's why the candleholders are so solid and stout; to guard against any possibility of falling over. And he's been told he must always and only put it on the wall shelf made for it set into the corner angle, not too low. It's to minimize the likelihood of anything falling onto the flame – a letter, a shirt sleeve – anything that could burn. Too many monasteries have gone up in flames.

Here in the south range, the light of the rising moon shines in on this clear night. The windows have glass – which feels very modern and aristocratic; those of the home he left behind had horn panes upstairs and just shutters below. The glass is uneven;

it's not possible to really see the stars. But the lower half of the window will open – and then you can. So he latches it open, because he loves the starlight.

After that, he climbs into bed and lies there thinking. His mind explores the idea of the scourge beneath his bed. Really? Will he ever do that? Should he? Might he even *want* to so subdue his flesh? Under what circumstances? If he'd been in Brother Damian's cell tonight he'd have got the picture.

Faintly, from somewhere nearby, he hears someone beginning to snore. Then he hears quiet feet pass his door, and the latch of the adjacent cell. Brother Cedd. What happened? Why did he go? Colin wonders if he'll ever find out. Brother Cedd is self-contained, reserved, certainly not chatty. He has never shown any inclination to bare his heart to Colin. Would it be permissible to ask him? Probably not.

It feels right, though, to have him back. Home, perhaps, is the place your feet take you – where you can't help but return; the place you are most yourself, in the loneliness of living. The place you belong.

An audacious idea comes to him. Greatly daring – he is not allowed to do this – he slips out of bed, creeps to the door, opens it as silently as he can, looks along the corridor both ways to be sure it is deserted, then taps lightly, just with his fingernails, not his knuckles, on the door of Brother Cedd's cell. Again. The small sound of movement inside ceases. His heart hammering in his throat – he knows this is entirely forbidden – his resolve evaporating, he taps once more. This time, the latch is quietly lifted within, and the door opens a fraction to reveal the warm glow of candlelight and Brother Cedd's surprised face checking if that really is someone knocking at his cell. Seeing Colin standing there, he opens the door a little more, his expression enquiring – *Yes?* – though he does not speak.

"Are you all right?" whispers Colin, and Brother Cedd's face relaxes into a smile. He nods, gives Colin a thumbs-up sign. "Thank you," he mouths silently.

As Colin returns to his own cell, outside the night wind is rising, blowing from the moor, and there's a distant rumble of thunder. Climbing back into bed, he curls onto his side, tugging the blanket up to keep the draft off his neck. He pictures Cedd's face, happy, no tell-tale signs of tears, his smile communicating appreciation of Colin's friendly gesture. That's all right, then. Gradually, peacefully, he drifts off to sleep.

✠ ✠ ✠

Shutting the door on the day as he comes in from the cloister to his house, the abbot takes the lantern, its light still burning, down from its safe hook jutting from the wall. Holding it so he can see, he considers the things half done awaiting his attention on the big table. Letters. Lists. Books for preparing the school catechetics class. But hey, who cares? It'll wait – all of it. The hours of the Silence, in truth, are meant for prayer and dreaming, not for work. This is God's time. And besides, he feels too happy. He wants to lie on his bed in the quiet dark and savour the joy of Cedd returning.

So he leaves the work lie until the morning, and carries the light through into his chamber. He sets it on the chest while he takes off his sandals, and his belt with his pocket, his rosary, his knife. He takes off his scapular and his cowl. Simple human in an ordinary black wool tunic, he kneels down to pray. And tonight his prayers are mainly, "Thank you... thank you... thank you..." Because a time comes to set formulae aside and reach out your hands to the God who is really there.

Then he reaches for the candle, blows it out, pinches the wick. He knows he shouldn't do this, knows he should use a snuffer. But there's a way – if you don't purse your lips and stream the air, if you just open your mouth and extinguish it with a small puff like the one God breathed into the clay he shaped to make Adam a living being – it's perfectly possible to do it without spraying the wax. He's always careful.

It's not easy, being abbot; sometimes it asks all he's got and a bit more that he has to have on account from Father God. But as he lays himself down on the straw mattress, moulded by this time surprisingly comfortably to his body's shape, contentment possesses him body and soul. He's tired, but it's been a good day.

✠ ✠ ✠

As Brother Tom closes the door to his cell, its familiar paradox makes itself felt. Its small dimensions make it feel safe and intimate; here he lets down his guard entirely, touches the presence of his Master. Yet the austerity of its simplicity lends a quality oddly spacious. As he knows from long experience, infinity can fit into this humble, whitewashed room.

He prefers to kneel on the floor by his bed, not at the priedieu. He stretches his arms across the blanket, his palms upraised. He does not speak aloud, but his soul calls out to God. *Look upon me... forgive me my sins... keep me close to thee... keep me in thy way... humble me... purify me... may I be always and always thy man, thy son, thy servant... watch over me this night... into thy hands, O Lord, I commend my spirit... thou hast redeemed me, Lord, I belong to thee...*

He's meant to keep the light burning, but he doesn't; he likes the restful dark. The bed creaks as he gets into it. He's putting on weight. Brother Conradus's doing, is that. Nobody got fat when Cormac was cook.

He lies in the coolness of night, his window ajar. Across the valley he hears the high, unmistakable yapping of a vixen, and he smiles, thinking of William setting down a bowl of bread and milk and abstracted scraps for his hungry fox. By heaven, how that man has changed. Thank God his brushes with death came to nothing. It just shows, you never know what's round the corner – there's always hope. Nobody is beyond redemption.

He wonders how things went between Abbot John and Brother Cedd. That's the great thing about John – you can trust him with people. He gets the best out of men. You couldn't call him a soft touch, but he hasn't a mean bone in his body. Kind, is John. He makes a good shepherd. Ooh – better tell him Nightmare's in the stable, and William will be up to fetch her back in the morning.

Tom draws in his breath in a yawn, and enjoys the feeling of stretching out, relaxing comfortably after a long day, a long ride. Cedd. He thinks about Brother Cedd. *Help him find his niche... peace be to his soul... may he –* But he's asleep before his mind completes its sentence.

✠ ✠ ✠

Ten miles away, at Caldbeck, their guests gone, the board cleared, the chores done, ashes swept over the embers and the beasts all abed, William and Madeleine stand there, just the two of them in the almost darkness, his arms around her.

She whispers, "Will you make love to me?"

"Oh..." He rubs the side of his face tenderly, slowly, against the top of her head. "With all my heart," he says.

✠ ✠ ✠

Now the abbey is wrapped in peace, withdrawn into Great Silence.

Good night. Go well. God be with you. Joy is there in the journeying. Keep the faith.

Glossary of Terms

Braies – Medieval term for underpants – made of linen, loose-fitting, with a drawstring or belt.

Calefactory – Also called the "warming room". The abbey's common room, with a big fireplace, for the community's relaxation in the hour before Compline.

Clepsydra – Water clock.

Custumals – Documents of medieval England, relating to such settlements as towns, manors, and monasteries, setting out their social, economic, and political customs and traditions, creating precedents which others could study and learn from.

Dorter – A dormitory, though by this point in the Middle Ages, monks slept in individual cells – retro-fitted wooden cubicles in the case of monasteries built back in the old days when they all shared one big room.

Horarium – Latin for "hours" – the occasions of liturgical worship dispersed through the monastic day.

Lavatorium – Though we take our modern word "lavatory" from here, and by it we mean "toilet", this word comes from the Latin for washing, and is not a toilet but a washroom.

Midden – Compost pile; general household dump.

Prie-dieu – Prayer-desk for private devotions.

Reredorter – Literally, "behind where we sleep": the toilets.

Vigils – The night Offices, sometimes called Nocturns. The Office of Vigils concludes with Matins, so in the course of time the night Office came to be known as Matins, and the daybreak Office, once Matins, became Lauds.

Monastic Day

There may be slight variation from place to place and at different times from the Dark Ages through the Middle Ages and onward – e.g., Vespers may be after supper rather than before. This gives a rough outline. Slight liberties are taken in my novels to allow human interactions to play out.

Winter Schedule (from Michaelmas)
2:30 a.m. Preparation for the nocturns of matins – psalms, etc.
3:00 a.m. Matins, with prayers for the royal family and for the dead.
5:00 a.m. Reading in preparation for Lauds.
6:00 a.m. Lauds at daybreak and Prime; wash and break fast (just bread and water, standing).
8:30 a.m. Terce, Morrow Mass, Chapter.
12:00 noon Sext, Sung Mass, midday meal.
2:00 p.m. None.
4:15 p.m. Vespers, Supper, Collatio.
6:15 p.m. Compline.
The Grand Silence begins.

Summer Schedule
1:30 a.m. Preparation for the nocturns of matins – psalms etc.
2:00 a.m. Matins.
3:30 a.m. Lauds at daybreak, wash and break fast.
6:00 a.m. Prime, Morrow Mass, Chapter.
8:00 a.m. Terce, Sung Mass.
11:30 a.m. Sext, midday meal.
2:30 p.m. None.
5:30 p.m. Vespers, Supper, Collatio.
8:00 p.m. Compline.
The Grand Silence begins.

Liturgical Calendar

I have included the main feasts and fasts in the cycle of the church's year, plus one or two other dates that are mentioned (e.g., Michaelmas and Lady Day when rents were traditionally collected) in these stories.

Advent – begins four Sundays before Christmas.

Christmas – December 25th.

Holy Innocents – December 28th.

Epiphany – January 6th.

Baptism of our Lord concludes Christmastide, Sunday after January 6th.

Candlemas – February 2nd (Purification of Blessed Virgin Mary, Presentation of Christ in the temple).

Lent – Ash Wednesday to Holy Thursday – start date varies with phases of the moon.

Holy Week – last week of Lent and the Easter Triduum.

Easter Triduum (three days) of Good Friday, Holy Saturday, Easter Sunday.

Lady Day – March 25th – this was New Year's Day between 1155 and 1752.

Ascension – forty days after Easter.

Whitsun (Pentecost) – fifty days after Easter.

Trinity Sunday – Sunday after Pentecost.

Corpus Christi – Thursday after Trinity Sunday.

Sacred Heart of Jesus – Friday of the following week.

Feast of John the Baptist – June 24th.

Lammas (literally "loaf-mass"; grain harvest) – August 1st.

Michaelmas – feast of St Michael and All Angels, September 29th.

All Saints – November 1st.

All Souls – November 2nd.

Martinmas – November 11th.